9 FROM THE NINE WORLDS

MAGNUS CHASE
and the GODS of ASGARD

9 FROM THE
NINE WORLDS

STORIES
BY
RICK RIORDAN

DISNEY • HYPERION
Los Angeles   New York

Illustrations by James Firnhaber, Jim Madsen, and Yori Elita Narpati

First Edition, October 2018
3 5 7 9 10 8 6 4 2
FAC-020093-18270
Printed in the United States of America

This book is set in 11-point New Baskerville, Adobe Caslon Pro, Danton,
Gauthier FY, Goudy, Goudy Trajan/Fontspring; Janson Text LT Pro/Monotype
Designed by Beth Meyers
Rune and symbol art by Michelle Gengaro-Kokmen

Library of Congress Cataloging-in-Publication Data
Names: Riordan, Rick, author.
Title: 9 from the Nine Worlds / Rick Riordan.
Other titles: Nine from the Nine Worlds
Description: First edition. • Los Angeles ; New York : Disney-Hyperion,
2018. • Series: Magnus Chase and the gods of Asgard • Summary: "Beloved
characters from the Magnus Chase and the Gods of Asgard series star in these
hilarious and inventive new short stories, each set in a different one of the Nine
Worlds from Norse mythology"— Provided by publisher. Includes glossary,
pronunciation guide, and list of runes.
Identifiers: LCCN 2017053123 • ISBN 9781368024044
Subjects: • CYAC: Mythology, Norse—Fiction. • Short stories.
Classification: LCC PZ7.R4829 Aaf 2018 • DDC [Fic]—dc23
LC record available at https://lccn.loc.gov/2017053123

Reinforced binding
Visit www.DisneyBooks.com

SUSTAINABLE Certified Sourcing
FORESTRY
INITIATIVE www.sfiprogram.org
SFI-00993

THIS LABEL APPLIES TO TEXT STOCK

A special thank-you to Stephanie True Peters
for her help with this book

CONTENTS

Asgard

Just Another Decapitated Head

BY ODIN

MY *EINHERJAR* have a saying: *Some days you are the ax, some days you are the decapitated head.* I like it so much, I'm having T-shirts made for the Hotel Valhalla gift shop.

As the All-Father, god of wisdom, king of the Aesir, and ruler of all Asgard, I am usually the ax. Strong. Powerful. In control.

Usually. But one day not long ago . . . well, let's just say things went awry.

It started when Hunding, bellhop of Valhalla, informed me of a disturbance in the Feast Hall of the Slain.

"Disturbance?" I asked as I opened the hall door.

Splat!

"A food fight, Lord Odin."

I peeled a slab of uncooked Saehrimnir from my cheek. "So I see."

It wasn't just any food fight. It was a Valkyrie food fight. Above me, a dozen or more airborne choosers of the slain swooped and dive-bombed while pelting one another with feast beast meat, potatoes, bread, and other edibles.

"Enough!"

My voice sent a shock wave through the hall. All fighting stopped.

"Drop your weapons."

Saehrimnir steaks and other foods hit the floor.

"Now clean up this mess and think about what you've done."

As the Valkyries moved to find mops, I beckoned to Hunding, who was cowering in a corner. "Walk with me."

We wove our way through Hotel Valhalla, the eternal home of my einherjar—mortals who had died heroically. My noble Valkyries are responsible for whisking the deceased here, where the brave warriors train to fight on the gods' side against the giants at Ragnarok, the Day of Doom. (If you wish to know more about this afterlife program, refer to my informational pamphlet *Dying to Fight*.)

I paused at the bottom of a stone staircase. "Since the death of Gunilla, captain of the Valkyries, some of my handmaidens have become . . . feisty." I touched my face where the raw meat had struck. "I had hoped the Valkyries would choose a new captain themselves. Since they have not, I must intervene."

Hunding looked relieved. "Do you have Gunilla's replacement in mind, Lord Odin?"

Sadly, I did not. My first choice, Samirah al-Abbas, had opted to become my Valkyrie in charge of special assignments instead. I had no second choice—yet.

"Tell the thanes to bring candidates to the Thing Room in one hour. I'll be scanning the Nine Worlds from Hlidskjalf if you need me. And, Hunding?"

"Yes, Lord Odin?"

"Don't need me."

I mounted the stairs to my pavilion and sank onto Hlidskjalf, the magic throne from which I can peer into the Nine Worlds. The seat cradled my posterior with its ermine-lined softness. I took a few deep breaths to focus my concentration, then turned to the worlds beyond.

I usually begin with a cursory look-see of my own realm, Asgard, then circle through the remaining eight: Midgard, realm of the humans; the elf kingdom of Alfheim; Vanaheim, the Vanir gods' domain; Jotunheim, land of the giants; Niflheim, the world of ice, fog, and mist; Helheim, realm of the dishonorable dead; Nidavellir, the gloomy world of the dwarves; and Muspellheim, home of the fire giants.

This time, I didn't make it past Asgard. Because goats.

Specifically, Thor's goats, Marvin and Otis. They were

on the Bifrost, the radioactive Rainbow Bridge that connects Asgard to Midgard, wearing footy pajamas. But there was no sign of Thor, which was odd. He usually kept Marvin and Otis close. He killed and ate them every day, and they came back to life the next morning.

More disturbing was Heimdall, guardian of the Bifrost. He was hopping around on all fours like a deranged lunatic. "So here's what I want you guys to do," he said to Otis and Marvin between hops. "Cavort. Frolic. Frisk about. Okay?"

I parted the clouds. "Heimdall! What the Helheim is going on down there?"

"Oh, hey, Odin!" Heimdall's helium-squeaky voice set my teeth on edge. He waved his phablet at me. "I'm making a cute baby goat video as my Snapchat story. Cute baby goat videos are *huge* in Midgard. *Huge!*" He spread his hands out wide to demonstrate.

"I'm not a baby!" Marvin snapped.

"I'm cute?" Otis wondered.

"Put that phablet away and return to your duties at once!"

According to prophecy, giants will one day storm across the Bifrost, a signal that Ragnarok is upon us. Heimdall's job is to sound the alarm on his horn, Gjallar—a job he would not be able to perform if he were making Snapchat stories.

"Can I finish my cute baby goat video first?" Heimdall pleaded.

"No."

"Aw." He turned to Otis and Marvin. "I guess that's a wrap, guys."

"Finally," Marvin said. "I'm going for a graze." He hopped off the bridge and plummeted to almost certain death and next-day resurrection. Otis sighed something about the grass being greener on the other side, then jumped after him.

"Heimdall," I said tightly, "need I remind you what could happen if even one jotun snuck into Asgard?"

Heimdall hung his head. "Apologetic face emoji."

I sighed. "Yes, all right. I—"

A movement in Hotel Valhalla's garden caught my eye. I looked closer. And immediately wished I hadn't.

Legs spraddled and wearing nothing but a pair of leather short-shorts, Thor was bending, twisting, and squat-farting. Strapped to his ankle was a device shaped like a *valknut*, a design of three interlocking triangles.

"What in the name of me is my son doing?" I asked in bewilderment.

"Who, Thor?" Heimdall looked over his shoulder. "He's warming up for a jog through the Nine Worlds."

"A jog. Through the Nine Worlds," I repeated.

"Yep. If he logs ten million steps on his FitnessKnut—that thing around his ankle—he earns a cameo appearance on a Midgard television show. That's why I had his goats. He said they'd slow him down."

"That's ridiculous!"

"Not really. Those goats aren't exactly speedy. Unless they're plummeting, that is."

"Not what I meant. . . . Never mind." I cupped my hands around my mouth. "Thor! *Thor!*"

Heimdall tapped his ears. "He's listening to rock."

"Rock 'n' roll?"

"No, just rock. Boulders, gravel, stones." Heimdall paused. "Or did he say the Stones?"

Thankfully, a messenger raven swooped into the pavilion just then to summon me to the thane meeting.

"At last," I muttered as I headed to the Thing Room. "A moment of sanity."

I opened the conference room door to find my trusted advisors twirling in their plush leather chairs.

"Whoever spins the longest without getting sick wins!" one of the Eriks yelled.

"Thanes!" I roared. "Come to order!"

My advisors quickly pulled their chairs to the table (except for Snorri Sturluson, who staggered to the nearest trash bin and threw up). I took my seat at the head and nodded at Hunding. "Bring forth the candidates."

The first nominee was Freydis, daughter of Erik the Red. Freydis had been a fine Valkyrie back in the day. But judging from her hunched back, vacant smile, and milky eyes, the years had not been kind to her.

"Erik," I observed, "your daughter is literally ancient."

Erik pointed at me with double finger spears. "Ancient equals experience, am I right?"

"Not in this case." I thanked Freydis for her past service and sent her hobbling on her way.

Next was Kara, a well-meaning but clumsy oaf who giggled incessantly. She'd only become a Valkyrie because of her centuries-old relationship with Helgi, manager of Hotel Valhalla. A nice girl? Yes. Worthy of leading my female warriors?

"Ah, no," I replied to Helgi's hopeful look.

Boudica, the fearsome queen of the Celts and a Valkyrie since the year 61, was Davy Crockett's choice. She barged in brandishing her sword, swept the room with an impatient glance, then flung her head back and shrieked with rage.

"I was told there would be snacks!" She beheaded the nearest floor lamp and stormed out.

I pinched the bridge of my nose. "At least the next candidate can't be any worse."

The next candidate was worse.

A decrepit crone with stringy gray hair and filthy, ragged robes shambled into the room. Her body odor hit me the same time recognition did. I shot out of my seat and summoned Gungnir, my magic spear. "You!"

The hag gave a phlegm-thick cackle. "Ooh, remember me, do you, ol' One-Eye?"

"I banished you from the Valkyries centuries ago!" I glared at my thanes. "Who dares drag this witch before me?"

"Oh, don't yell at them," she chided. "When I heard you were choosing a new Valkyrie captain, I couldn't resist showing up." She coughed up something nasty into her palm and wiped it on her robes.

"Begging your pardon, Lord Odin," Hunding whispered, "but who is she?"

"Hladgunnr," I growled. "Daughter of Hel, granddaughter of Loki. She plagued Valhalla with her tricks."

Hladgunnr whooped. "Remember that time I left a trail of nuts to lead Ratatosk to Laeradr?"

"That was *you*?" Snorri cried. "The squirrel's insults soured Heidrun's milk mead!" He buried his face in his hands. "Dinner was *ruined*!"

"What can I say?" She winked at me. "Pranks are my thing." The air around her rippled, and she began to shrink.

Alarm bells rang in my head. "Hladgunnr inherited Loki's deceitful ways, not his power to shape-shift."

Screeching with laughter, the imposter transformed into a bald eagle.

"Utgard-Loki." A current of fear spread through the thanes when I spoke the name of the king of the mountain giants. I thrust the business end of Gungnir at the bird. "How did you gain entrance to this world?"

The eagle leered. "An unexpected opportunity presented itself. I took it."

I grimaced. "Heimdall and his baby goat video."

"I'm not a baby!" Marvin yelled from somewhere outside the hotel.

"And Hladgunnr?" I demanded.

"She came to me when you banished her. Horrible BO, but a great source of intel, right up to the end. *Her* end, that is." Utgard-Loki drew a wing tip across his throat. "Impersonating her was a cinch. Embarrassing you in front of your thanes? That was an added bonus."

I'd heard enough. I reared back and threw my spear. It never misses, yet Gungnir sailed past the eagle. How . . . ?

Utgard-Loki crowed with laughter. "The mighty Odin, foiled by a bit of distortion magic? This *is* a good day!"

I blinked and saw the eagle was no longer on the table— perhaps it never had been—but by an open window. He saluted me with a wing, then soared off toward the distant mountains of Jotunheim.

I sank into my chair. "Clear the room."

The thanes beat a hasty retreat. In the silence that followed, one thought rolled through my mind: *Some days you are the ax, some days you are the decapitated head.*

I'd never felt more decapitated in my life. I didn't like it. So, I chose to become the ax.

"Hunding, stop skulking in the hallway and get in here."

The bellhop poked his head around the doorway. "I wasn't skulking," he said defensively. "I was lingering."

"Come in. I need you to do three things. One: Find a

way to track Thor's FitnessKnut. Report his whereabouts at all times."

"Won't he just circle the worlds in order?"

I made a face. "Thor's sense of direction is terrible. His path will likely be erratic. Moving on. Two: Have squads of einherjar launch surprise attacks on the Bifrost. I want to know that Heimdall is on guard."

"Very good, sir. And the third thing?"

"Inform the thanes that as of tomorrow, I will be unavailable for a while." I transformed my appearance from a rugged one-eyed god of wisdom to a beautiful two-eyed woman clad in chain mail. "I will be living with my Valkyries to decide for myself which of them deserves to be captain."

Hunding raised a hairy eyebrow. "An idea from Utgard-Loki, Lord Odin?"

"Wisdom can be gleaned from any source if one only looks hard enough." I paused, thinking. "Let's put that on a T-shirt. And, Hunding?"

"My lord?"

I transformed back into my true form. "Download cute baby goat videos to my phablet. I must learn what all the fuss is about."

MIDGARD

This Is Why I Hate Clothes Shopping

BY AMIR FADLAN

"AMIR, YOU look hideous." My fiancée, Samirah al-Abbas, stared at my outfit in horrified disbelief.

"Really?" I looked down at myself. "But it's a tux!"

"A baby-blue tux!"

"With a matching ruffled shirt and floppy bow tie," I said defensively. "My uncle loaned it to me. I think it'll impress your grandparents, don't you?"

"It's Jid and Bibi's fiftieth wedding anniversary!" Sam sputtered. "You can't wear—"

"Samirah." My father emerged from the kitchen. "He is pulling your leg."

Sam's reddish-brown eyes blazed dangerously, and I

suddenly realized that playing a practical joke on a Valkyrie might not be the best idea I ever had.

"I'm heading over to Blitzen's shop right now," I hastily reassured her. "I'll pick out something appropriate, I promise."

"I'll go with you, just to be sure," Sam said.

My father cleared his throat and raised his eyebrows.

"Don't worry, Dad," I said. "Blitz will be there to chaperone us."

"Good to know," my father replied. "But I was actually going to suggest you change before you leave."

"Oh. Right. Give me five minutes."

I ran up to my room and began undressing. Then I froze. Out of the corner of my eye, I saw a shadow move across my window. Someone was on the fire escape. The hair on the back of my neck stood up. Heart pounding, I tiptoed over and inched open the curtain.

A pigeon swooped past my face. I leaped back, tripped, and landed on my butt.

"Stupid bird," I muttered. I quickly swapped the tux for faded jeans and a white T-shirt, then hurried back downstairs.

Sam was on her cell phone. *Odin*, she mouthed at me. She listened for a moment, then hung up and gave me an apologetic look. "I have to go. A last-minute einherji extraction. It shouldn't take too long. I'll meet you at Blitzen's. Don't buy anything until I get there!"

I walked her to the door. Sam looked left and right, then leaped into the air and flew off.

"I will never get used to that," I murmured.

Unlike most mortals, I can see through the glamour, the magical force that disguises reality. I can thank—or curse—Magnus Chase for making that possible. He thought it best that I know about my fiancée's Valkyrie life. I wondered what my father would have made of Sam's sudden disappearance. A superfast Uber pickup, maybe?

Having my mind open this way wasn't always fun. For example, on my way to Blitzen's Best, I passed Thor. I saw him for what he really was: a sweaty muscle-bound redheaded deity in leather shorts that left little to the imagination. Though the way other pedestrians hurriedly moved aside, it's possible they caught a glimpse of the real Thor, too.

Blitzen's Best, the upscale clothing store owned and operated by Sam's dwarf friend, helped erase the image of Thor from my brain. I'm not much of a clotheshorse—*just say no to the hipster man-bun look* was my motto—but Blitz's colorful designs spoke to me. They didn't seem to call to anyone else, though. I was alone in the store.

"Hey, Blitz, you here?"

A thin man with close-set eyes, patchy light brown hair, and a sparse mustache emerged from the back room. He curled his hands against his chest, like a rodent squatting on its haunches. "The dwarf is not in right now," he informed me in a thin, reedy voice. "I am Stan. May I help you with your purchase?"

To me, shopping for clothes meant grabbing the right size of jeans from a lopsided pile. I wasn't used to having a salesman offer to help, and I'd never known Blitz to have an employee. Then again, I was on Newbury Street, home of Boston's most exclusive boutiques, where customers expected personal service. So I went along, cautiously.

"Sure, I guess." I selected a pair of dark blue trousers from a nearby rack. "I'm going to a fiftieth anniversary party, so I'm looking for something special to wear."

"Special. Yes." He took the trousers from me and returned them to the rack. "These are not special."

I was pretty sure Blitzen would disagree, but I didn't say anything.

Stan wrung his hands as his beady eyes darted over my frame. "Just as I thought. You are trim. Tall, but not too tall. Your legs are slender." He looked up at me. "I have something special that will fit you like a second skin. Wait here."

I'm not going to lie. When Stan disappeared into the back room, I almost bolted. The guy gave off a seriously weird vibe. But the party was that night. If I didn't get something in this store, I'd end up wearing the blue tux. Better to risk Stan's weirdness over Sam's wrath.

Stan returned with a pair of light tan leather pants. He caressed the material, which was unlike any leather I'd ever seen. "Try these." He extended his arms, giving me no choice but to take the pants. "Put them on, and you will never take them off."

"Uh, I hope you mean I'll never *want* to take them off," I corrected.

"You will wear them *forever!*"

Stan's voice had taken on a feverish edge that made me regret not bolting. I decided to appease him by trying on the pants. I'd claim they didn't fit or were too expensive or something, and get out of there quick.

I held up the pants to examine them in the bright lights of the dressing room. They looked formfitting, like skinny jeans, tapered at the ankle and snug through the hips and thighs. The peculiar leather was lightweight and papery in feel. They were slip-on, with no zipper, just a single ivory button at the waist. Poking out of the single deep front pocket was a scrap of wrinkled yellow paper with a symbol scrawled in red-brown ink.

"You have not put them on yet."

I nearly jumped out of my skin. Stan was just outside the curtain. I hadn't heard him approach.

"Uh, one sec." I shoved the paper back into the pocket, kicked off my sneakers, and slipped out of my jeans. My cell phone fell to the floor. I debated texting Samirah to tell her to hurry up, then remembered she was doing her Valkyrie thing. I put my phone back in my jeans and laid them on the dressing room bench. Then I stepped into the tan pants, pulled them up, and fastened the button.

Vvvvtttt! With a sound like a vacuum nozzle sucking against a piece of paper, the pants suddenly constricted around my body.

"Hey! What the heck?"

The curtain flew open. Stan stood there, circling his hands in the air. "You have put them on. Willingly. With your own hands."

"Yeah, and now I'm taking them off. Immediately. With force!" My fingers scrabbled at the button, but it wouldn't unfasten. I shoved my thumbs into the waistline and tried to wriggle free. The leather stuck to me as if it had been painted on. I yanked at the ankles, clawed at the sides. The pants didn't budge or tear.

"The pocket. Check the pocket!" Stan stared at the pants, which did nothing to ease my growing alarm.

"There's nothing in it but an old piece of paper."

Stan stepped closer. "Check. Again." He enunciated each word in a voice no longer thin and reedy, but deranged and dangerous. *"Now!"*

"Okay, okay, chill out! I'm checking." I slipped my hand inside and blinked. My fingers touched a coin. A half dollar, judging by the size. I withdrew it and gulped. "Is this . . . *gold?*"

Stan thrust out his cupped hands. "Give it to me."

Dazed, I dropped it into his palms.

"The pocket," Stan whispered. "Again."

I pulled out a second gold coin. Then a third and a fourth. As soon as I removed one, another took its place. Within seconds, gold coins were spilling from Stan's hands onto the floor. He crouched and started running his fingers through the glittering pile.

I edged toward the front of the store. "Okay, well, this has been fun, and you're obviously busy, so if you could tell me how to take off the pants, I'll be on my way."

"You cannot go," Stan said, still playing Mr. Moneybags with the coins. "Not as long as you wear the *nábrók*."

"*Nábrók*? What does that mean?"

Stan glanced at me and smiled slowly. "Necropants."

I blanched. I'd seen enough crime dramas to know that the prefix *necro* meant *death*. "Just to be clear, *nábrók* means *death pants*?" I swallowed hard. "Are they going to kill me?"

"No. You misunderstand."

Relief flooded me. "For a moment there, I thought—"

"Nábrók are pants made from the skin of a dead person."

I clapped my hands over my mouth to keep from vomiting.

"These necropants have been in my family for generations," Stan went on. "They were created by my ancestor, a mighty sorcerer skilled in dark magic. The symbol on the paper is a powerful spell written in the blood of the deceased. The spell . . . it makes gold coins. Forever."

"Then take the paper!" I cried. "I don't want it."

"Fool!" Stan shot to his feet. "The spell must remain in the pocket. It is activated only when a male descendant of the dead man willingly and by his own hand fits the pants onto his body."

"A male descendant?" Horror flooded my veins. "You mean these are—?"

"Made from the skin of your ancestor, yes."

"Ahh!" I desperately clawed at the pants. I didn't want to wear my great-grandfather or anyone else. But they were invulnerable.

Stan's eyes gleamed. "I've been watching you, Amir Fadlan, waiting for my chance to give them to you."

I remembered the shadow crossing my window and once again almost vomited. "Where's Blitzen? What have you—?"

Ding-a-ling!

The bell over the store's front door jangled. "Amir? Blitzen? Anybody?" a voice asked. "Jeez, I could rob this place blind and no one would know it."

I sucked in my breath. *Alex.*

Alex Fierro was a gender-fluid einherji from Hotel Valhalla and Samirah's half sibling. He sounded male at the moment—and a little annoyed.

"You know this person." Stan said it to me like a statement, not a question. "If you value their life, you will remain quiet. I too know how to wield dark magic." He gave me a warning look, rearranged his expression to pleasant, and hurried out front. "Good afternoon. May I be of assistance?"

I had a partial view of Alex through the curtain. In his eye-catching pink-and-green outfit and dyed-green hair, he looked more at home in Blitzen's Best than I ever would. But he didn't see me, and I didn't dare draw his attention. Stan obviously had more nasty surprises up his sleeve.

"Who are you?" Alex asked. "Where's Blitz?"

"I am Stan. The dwarf has gone to his apartment to retrieve necessary fashion supplies."

Alex leaned an elbow on the counter. "Stan, huh? Well, Stan, I'm looking for a guy who came here to buy an outfit for a fiftieth wedding anniversary. Tall, fit, and attractive, with a faint scent of falafel. Has he been in?"

"I have seen no such person."

"Well, maybe I could pick out something for him. Heck, I might get a few things for myself, too."

"No. We are closing now. Good day." Stan moved to the door and opened it for Alex.

"Sheesh, hold your horses, pal! I gotta call his fiancée first." Alex pulled out his cell phone and thumbed a number.

A muffled ringtone sounded from my jeans on the dressing room bench—Alex's ringtone. He was calling my phone. But if I answered it, Stan might put a spell on—

"Whoops, wrong number." Alex hung up and dialed again. "Samirah? Yeah, I'm at Blitz's. This guy Stan says the dwarf isn't here and that Amir hasn't been in. He won't sell me anything, because they're closing, like, right now."

Alex listened for a moment, then laughed. "Oh, *definitely*

bring that, so when you see him, you can let him have it."

What did Alex mean by "that"? I wondered.

Alex hung up. "She is *so* not happy."

"You will leave now."

"Yeah, yeah."

Alex pushed off the counter and sauntered out. Stan locked the store door and returned to the dressing room. Without warning, he grabbed my arm and twisted it behind my back. Pain exploded in my shoulder.

"It is time to go."

"Go where?"

"No need to worry about that, my pet," said Stan, "as that is exactly what you are now—my pet."

Going anyplace with him seemed like a very, very bad idea. Stalling, on the other hand, seemed like a terrific plan. "Wait! What about the gold? Shouldn't we—you—bring it?"

Stan laughed. "The nábrók will give an abundant supply. Endless."

"Can't I at least put my jeans back on? They'll fit over the—the necropants." I almost lost my lunch saying the word. "And hide them from prying eyes."

"Who would notice?" Stan scoffed.

"Heimdall." The guardian's name just popped into my head. With his far-seeing gaze, he could spot trouble in the Nine Worlds—when he wasn't gazing at his phablet. "He and I have a special connection. He even took a selfie with me."

Stan paused, considering. "Very well." He released my arm. "But don't try anything foolish."

Naturally, I tried something foolish. Instead of putting on my jeans, I snatched up the nearest weapon—my left sneaker—and whipped it at his head.

With one lightning-quick move, Stan caught my sneaker in one hand and recaptured my arm with the other. "A shoe?" he growled. "Who throws a shoe? Honestly!" He shoved me through the curtain and then stopped short.

Sam stood in the middle of the store. With a spear of brilliant light in hand and wearing a suit of chain mail with a helmet over her green hijab, she looked drop-dead dangerous. If our religion didn't forbid it, I would have kissed her.

"Let him go." Sam's voice radiated Valkyrie power. "Amir belongs to me."

My heart swelled with pride. I felt like we could take on the whole world together, and—

"Not anymore," Stan snarled. "As long as he wears the nábrók, he is bound to *me*."

Oh.

Sam looked confused for a second. I pointed helplessly at my pants. She nodded and said, "Well, then we'll just have to unbind him!"

I heard a zinging sound behind me. Stan stiffened and dropped my arm like a hot potato. I spun to find Alex holding one end of his golden garrote like a leash. The other end was wrapped tightly around Stan, pinning his arms to his sides. Stan spit out a string of curse words.

"Oh, put a sock in it." Sam grabbed a pair of argyles and stuffed them into Stan's mouth.

Alex, meanwhile, eyed my legs. "Nice pants."

"Yeah, not really." I told them the disgusting truth about my attire.

"Gross," Alex said.

"There's more." I showed them the paper with the spell on it.

Sam grimaced. "Dark magic. I hate dark magic. *Light* magic, though . . ." She touched the tip of her spear to the paper and it vanished in a puff of bloodred smoke. "Light magic comes in handy."

Stan let out a muffled howl of fury.

"Hey, Amir." Alex pointed at the necropants. "Let's shuck 'em."

"Alex!" Sam cried, blushing.

Alex rolled his eyes. "I meant get them off—in the back room, obviously," he added when Sam blushed an even deeper shade of red. "Here, you hold Stan's leash."

He gave Sam his end of the garrote, took her spear, and followed me into the dressing room. He raised his eyebrows at the pile of gold coins, then turned to me. "Hold still."

"What are you— *Hey!*"

With three quick and too-close-for-comfort flicks of the

spear tip, Alex slashed the pants from my legs. I guess the light magic overpowered the dark once again. The pieces crumbled into drifts of dead skin, which slowly disintegrated into dust.

"Huh. That's not something you see every day," Alex said. Then he glanced at my boxers and made a face. "Or those." He tossed me my jeans and turned his back so I could dress in semiprivate.

"What tipped you off—about Stan, I mean?" I asked.

"Couple of things," Alex replied. "He referred to Blitzen as *the dwarf* and claimed you hadn't been in. Knowing how terrified you are of Sam—"

"I am not!"

"—I thought it was unlikely you'd skipped the shopping spree. So, I tested his story and called your phone. When I heard my ringtone, I knew he was lying about you being here. But the biggest clue? He refused to sell me anything. I mean, come on." He gestured to his pink cashmere sweater vest and tight lime-green pants. "A real clothing salesman would have seen dollar signs the minute I walked into the store." He nudged the gold coins with his rose-colored boot. "But I guess he had all the money he needed."

"And more where that came from." I shuddered. "He was going to use me as his own private ATM. Forever."

"Dude." Alex laid a comforting hand on my shoulder. "That would have sucked."

"If you boys are ready," Sam called, "I'd like to phone Blitzen, make sure he's okay. I want to check in with Odin, too. He'll know what to do with this creep."

"Hang on." I scooped up the coins from the floor. "I'm taking these for the Chase Space," I told Alex, referring to our friend Magnus's shelter for homeless children. "Anonymous donation for the kiddos. Except for this one." I put a coin on the counter by the register, then grabbed the dark blue trousers, a pink silk shirt, and a matching paisley vest. Samirah chose my tie.

"I still think I rocked that blue tux," I told her as we bagged my purchases.

"Oh, Amir." She smiled sweetly and leaned in close, making my heart thump. "If you ever wear that again," she whispered, "I'll skin you alive."

NIDAVELLIR

This Little Light of Mine, I'm Going to Let It Shine

BY BLITZEN

GATHERING SUPPLIES from my apartment in Nidavellir was the first item on my day's agenda. Not on that agenda? Fleeing an angry dwarf in a jet-propelled wheelchair. And yet there I was, racing through the dark streets of my home world with Eitri Junior, my old enemy (and I do mean *old*— the guy was one step shy of fossilization), in hot pursuit. Apparently, he was still miffed because I beat him in a recent crafting contest. Or because I won by sabotaging his handiwork. Either way, he was a sore loser.

"I'm gaining on you!" he wheezed. "I'm— *Aahhh!*"

Junior's scream was joined by the squeal of burning rubber. He whizzed by me in a blur, clinging to the wheelchair's armrests as if his life depended on it. Which perhaps it did, as he seemed out of control. Correction: He was most definitely out of control.

Boom! Junior crashed headlong into an unlit forge. The chair bounced back and toppled over, wheels spinning and jets sputtering in the dirt. Junior looked dazed, but unhurt. Dwarves came running from every direction.

That was my cue to leave. I still needed some things from my apartment, but I didn't go there. If Junior came after me again, that'd be the first place he'd look. What he might do if he found me . . . well, let's just say vengeance-seeking dwarves usually hack first and ask questions never, and I wasn't wearing my chain mail vest.

Darting from one alley to another, I zigzagged my way through a maze of unfamiliar streets. At one point, I fell face-first in a mud puddle, totally ruining my lavender overcoat. When I finally stopped to catch my breath, I was in a part of Nidavellir I'd never been before. It reminded me of a sketchy section of downtown Boston I'd warned Magnus to avoid.

I put up my collar and started walking. Asking for directions to my neighborhood was out. The few dwarves I passed either avoided making eye contact or rudely mocked my mud-soaked coat. To be fair, they would have mocked it even if it were clean. No appreciation for fashion, dwarves.

I came to a windowless tavern. Muffled pinging and

dinging sounds came from within. Not my first choice of sanctuary, but better than roaming the streets aimlessly. I ducked inside.

The interior was dimly lit even by Nidavellir standards, except for the row of pachinko machines. A cross between a vertical pinball game and a coin-operated gumball dispenser, they blinked and flashed with garish colored lights that clashed horribly with the dark wood and red-checkered décor. Seeing those games brought back painful memories of someone I was once connected to—and hoped to stay disconnected from. And then there was the smell—it took all of my willpower not to press my pocket square to my nose as I took a seat at the bar.

The bartender stood at the far end, polishing the inside of a brass mug. I raised a finger to get his attention.

"Hey, pal, I don't suppose you could tell me how to get to Kenning Square from here?"

He spat into the mug, then continued wiping it with his filthy rag. "Play, drink, or get out."

"Play? Oh, you mean pachinko. The thing is, I'm not much of a gambler."

"Play, drink, or get out."

"I'm not much of a drinker, either."

"Play, drink, or—"

The door banged open and a sour-faced dwarf came in. My heart plummeted. He was one of Junior's cronies.

I slid off the stool. "You know what? I think I'll play." I hurried to a machine tucked away in a corner and inserted a coin.

The game board went dark. "What the—?"

An extremely short but strong-looking dwarf emerged from the shadows. The machine's power cord dangled from his hand.

"You owe me a quarter," I said huffily.

The minuscule muscleman stepped closer and menaced my midriff with a scowl. "Someone wants to see you," he said.

I cut my eyes toward the front of the bar, where Junior's henchman was questioning the bartender. "If it's that guy, I'm not interested."

The burly dwarf glared up at me, then kicked open a hidden door next to the machine and stepped aside. "In back. Now."

I would have refused, except I heard the bartender say, "Yeah, he's here. Now play, drink, or get out."

"Right. In back. Now." I darted through the opening. The door closed with a quiet click behind me.

The back room was as dimly lit as the bar. A massive oak desk—beautifully carved, clearly a one-of-a-kind piece— took up much of the space. Behind it was a hand-tooled leather chair with brass rivets, its back to me.

"Um, hello?" I ventured. "You wanted to see me?"

The chair rotated with agonizing slowness. I held my breath, waiting to see who sat in it. It was empty.

"Ha-ha, very funny. You got me—whoever you are."

Laughter gurgled from the side wall. A light suddenly blazed, illuminating a large fish tank. There were no fish in it, though. Just a severed, bearded head bobbing in the water next to a plastic treasure chest.

I groaned. "Mimir. I should have known."

Mimir, an ancient god and my sometime employer, had a body once. Then he tried to pull a fast one on the Vanir. He dispensed wise advice through Honir, the god of indecision, and made them think he was a sage. When the Vanir discovered the deception, they decapitated Mimir. He survived from the neck up thanks to Odin's magic and the waters of the well of knowledge at the roots of Yggdrasil. He can usually be found there still, dishing out intel to supplicants in exchange for their servitude. I'd been his servant for a few years (long story), but even now that I was free, he still sometimes showed up in other bodies of water, usually to make my life miserable.

The head bobbed to the surface. "Hey, Blitz," Mimir said. "Long time no see. Pull up a seat. We got things to discuss. That's why I brought you here."

"What do you mean, brought me here?"

Mimir chuckle-bubbled. "A little wheelchair sabotage, a little magical manipulation of certain alleyways, bada-bing, bada-boom, and here you are. So, take a seat and have a listen."

I drew myself up to my full five feet five inches. "Odin freed me from your service, remember?"

Mimir sloshed with annoyance. "Yeah, yeah, yeah. Thing is, the worlds might be in trouble if you don't act on what I'm about to tell you. *Now* you interested in what I got to say?"

I huffed as I sat in the leather chair. *Why me?* "I'm listening."

"Right. You ever heard of a dwarf named Alviss?"

"No."

"Nasty piece of work. Anyway, he's plotting to kill Thor on account of Alviss was supposed to marry Thor's daughter, Thrud. Only Thor changed his mind at the last minute and petrified the guy instead. Someone fixed Alviss up with a little water, so now he is back to normal, and he is *peeved*. When he found out Thor was heading to Nidavellir on his jog through the Nine Worlds—"

"Thor's jog through . . . ?" I held up a hand. "Never mind. It's Thor. I should know better than to ask."

"As I was saying, Alviss is planning to take his revenge." Mimir floated down to the treasure chest and, using his chin, pressed a button to open it. Out popped a card, which he grabbed in his teeth, brought back to the surface, and offered to me.

I removed it gingerly from between his chompers. It was a plastic laminated map of Nidavellir.

"See that *X*?" Mimir asked. "My sources say that's where Alviss will attack. Be there. Stop him. I estimate you've got two hours to come up with a plan to save the thunder god."

"Me, save Thor?" I scoffed. "He can take care of himself!"

Mimir did a spit take. "You don't get it! You've gotta do the job without letting Thor realize he was ever in danger. That means zero contact with the thunder god. You can't even call out his name. If he finds out about Alviss, he could get mad enough to zap *all* the dwarves—*boom!*"

Before I could ask further questions, like why his sources couldn't deal with Alviss themselves, Mimir yanked a plug at the bottom of the tank with his teeth and was sucked down the drain, leaving me with a dripping map and no idea what to do. And I was still out a quarter from the pachinko machine.

At least I got back to my apartment safely, thanks to directions from the minuscule dwarf thug. Once inside, I studied the map. I recognized the *X*'s location, a steep cliff overlooking a river I had once fallen into with my buddy Hearthstone. We'd washed up in Mimir's well of knowledge, which was how we ended up bound in service to him in the first place.

Knowing the *X*'s location was the plus in the situation. On the minus side, the only way I could think of to stop

Alviss—aside from killing or maiming him, which I was not going to do; I had enough enemies in Nidavellir already—would be to replicate what Thor did and petrify Alviss. Then I could revive him with fresh running water once the thunder god was out of danger.

There was just one catch: petrification required sunlight, something Nidavellir lacked.

Okay, two catches: if the sunlight hit me, I'd turn into a statue, too. A well-dressed one, but still . . .

I paced the apartment. Made myself a snack. Paced some more. Checked the time. Panicked. Paced some more.

"Sunlight. Where am I going to get sunlight?"

I searched the room for inspiration. I picked up an expand-o-duck, my handcrafted metal figurine that thwarted enemies by growing to immense size and crushing them. Would it solve my problem with Alviss, though? I didn't think so.

Still holding the duck, my gaze landed on Hearthstone's tanning bed. My elf friend used its simulated sunlight to keep him healthy when he came to visit. I looked from the duck to the bed and back again. Suddenly, the wheels in my brain started turning.

"What if I built a smaller version of the tanning bed," I asked the duck, "but tweaked the light so that instead of a soft warm glow, it shot out a powerful concentrated beam of sunlight when I opened it? That could work, right?" I made the duck nod, then got busy.

Forty-five minutes later, I had crafted a perfect handheld replica of Hearth's bed. When I opened the clamshell—away from my face—a burst of brilliant sunlight shone out. I quickly snapped it shut again. "Probably not going to be a big seller in Nidavellir," I acknowledged. "But, hopefully, it'll do the trick."

With no time to lose, I selected a stylish ninja outfit from my closet—fitted dark jeans and a black cashmere hoodie with a front pocket for the mini bed—and hurried to the riverside. I hid myself in the shadows.

But either Alviss was a no-show or Mimir's sources were wrong, because no one else, angry dwarf or jogging god, was anywhere in sight.

Or so I thought.

Scritch-scritch.

Nidavellir is an underground world with domed cavern ceilings overhead instead of sky. The scratching sound had come from above me. I looked up and saw a dwarf clinging to a stalactite. One end of a rope was wrapped around his waist. The other was attached to a second stalactite far in front of him and directly over the street where Thor was likely to run. Jammed in Alviss's belt was a club bigger than he was.

It didn't take a genius to figure out his plan: swing down like a pendulum and club Thor on the head.

This presented my plan with two unanticipated problems. One, I wasn't sure how far my sunbeam would shoot.

The Nidavellir darkness might swallow it before it reached Alviss on the ceiling. I'd have to wait for him to swing down. That meant hitting a moving target. Problem number two, assuming I petrified the dwarf, I had to be sure he swung past or over Thor, not into him.

Then a third problem arose. The ground started shaking with measured thuds, which meant I'd run out of time.

"Thor." Alviss's furious whisper echoed off the cavern walls.

Heart pounding, I pulled out the mini bed. The footfalls drew closer. Thor thundered around a bend in the distance. The sight of him in his tighty-leatherys almost made me root for Alviss.

"Rock, rock. Rock-rock-rock. Rock, rock. Rock-rock-rock," Thor muttered in a loud monotone.

Eyes glued to Alviss, I got into a crouch. Thor drew nearer. I huffed a few quick breaths to psych myself up. Then—

"Aaaiiiii!" With a triumphant yell, Alviss let go of the stalactite. At the same time, I launched myself into Thor's path. I tucked, rolled, and caught a horrifying glimpse of his leather-clad god parts a split second before he tripped over me.

"Rock. Rock. Rock-rock-*whoa!*"

Thor pitched forward just as Alviss flew overhead, swinging for the fences. The dwarf's club swished through empty air. Thor righted himself and kept going. "Rock. Rock. Rock-rock-rock. . . ."

I'd broken the "zero contact" instruction, but the thunder god seemed oblivious to my presence, so no harm done. As for the killer dwarf—

"Noooooo!"

Flailing his club, Alviss reached the swing's high point and came screaming—literally—back. I opened the mini bed.

Zot! Alviss's scream cut off. I watched as the now petrified dwarf sailed past.

I know what it's like to be petrified. It stinks. So I had every intention of cutting Alviss free on his next pass-by and then dipping him in the river to restore him. But before I could, the stalactite attached to the rope broke. Alviss's momentum carried him over the cliff edge. He landed with a splash in the water below.

"Oops." I peered down, then waved my hand dismissively. "Ah, he'll be fine."

"Blitzen!" Junior suddenly appeared. He crutched toward me with his rocket-powered walker and a lot of friends. "Get him, boys!"

"Ha! Eat light, Junior!" I unleashed the power of the mini bed.

Sadly, instead of a turn-you-to-stone laser beam, a weak glow enveloped Junior like a soft blanket. The charge had run out. A thin crust formed around him. It was nowhere near as dramatic as instant petrification, but it was startling enough to make the other dwarves pause.

And that made me think about how I looked to them. A dwarf who handcrafts a weapon that petrifies other dwarves? Not cool.

"Listen!" I yelled. "My argument is with Junior, not you. When he decrustifies, tell him I want to talk."

I put the mini bed on the ground and showed them my empty hands while slowly backing away.

It would have been a very powerful moment if I hadn't backed off the cliff into the river. As I thrashed through the churning water toward shore, three things occurred to me. One, Junior would never, ever forgive me. Two, my cashmere hoodie was ruined. And three . . . Mimir owed me a lot more than a quarter.

ALFHEIM

Speaking of Trolls . . .

BY HEARTHSTONE

"READY FOR the next one?"

I lip-read T.J.'s question and nodded. He slid a flash card with a handwritten swear word on it across the table, then watched me with gleeful anticipation.

Smiling faintly, I opened my mind and focused on the *dagaz* runestone in my hand. Magic flowed through me like water through a pebbled stream. The stone warmed, and I signed the swear. I felt sound vibrations in the air, then T.J. fell back onto his bed, shaking with laughter.

I gave him a look and signed three words: *Pull yourself together.*

"Right. Sorry." T.J. grinned. "It's just . . . hearing cuss

words come out of thin air like that cracks me up every time."

I've never heard the sound of voices. I've rarely uttered a sound, either, aside from the occasional sharp intake of breath. Communication had never been a problem, however. My closest friends, Blitzen, Magnus, and Sam, knew ASL—Alf Sign Language—so we conversed easily. When the need arose, they translated for me.

But now I was spending more time in Hotel Valhalla. Many einherjar didn't know or seem interested in learning ASL (except for T.J., who felt that he needed to learn more curses in order to keep up with Halfborn and Mallory). Blitz, Magnus, and Sam weren't always around to translate, and I had an intense dislike for writing down my words for others to read. Because reasons.

So, I came up with a different way to communicate: rune magic using dagaz, the symbol meaning new beginnings and transformations, to convert my signs into spoken words.

I touched my tightly closed fingertips together: *More*.

T.J. nodded and slid over another card. I'd just opened my mind when he broke my concentration by tapping my leg. He pointed to a thin gold band around my wrist and asked, "Why's it doing that?"

The band was a gift from Inge, a lovely hulder—a woodland being, like a sprite, with a cow's tail and minor magical powers. Inge had once served my family in Alfheim. Been

enslaved by, more accurately. I had released her from service the first moment I could. In return, she had made me
the bracelet with strands of her hair. She and the band were
connected by magic, she had explained. If I were ever in
trouble, the bracelet would send her a signal. Likewise, I
would know she needed help if the bracelet was twinkling.

The bracelet was twinkling.

Alarmed, I leaped to my feet and shoved the dagaz rune
into my pocket. T.J. grabbed my arm. "Hearth! Is everything okay?"

I shook my head and pulled myself free. T.J. deserved
more of an explanation, but there wasn't time. I had to get
to Alfheim.

I grabbed my rune bag and raced across the hall to
Magnus's room. Inside was an atrium with direct access to
Yggdrasil, the World Tree. I swung up into its branches and
climbed to the nearest entrance to my home world. The last
thing I saw before I slipped through was T.J. staring up at
me in confusion.

Then I was floating through the intense sunlight of my
world. Far below was the weed-choked rubble heap that was
once my childhood home. I willed myself to shift direction
away from it. Not because I regretted its destruction—quite
the opposite; the place conjured up nothing but unhappy
memories—but because I knew Inge would be elsewhere.
And wherever she was, she was in trouble. The bracelet
conveyed that much with its frantic twinkling. She'd been

captured, I feared, and enslaved as she had once been by my family.

I landed on an immaculate patch of grass in a picturesque park. The shade trees, duck ponds, trimmed hedges—everything around me screamed perfection, like most things in Alfheim. I kicked up a divot just to leave a blemish, then set off to find Inge.

There was just one problem: Alfheim was vast. Wealthy estates like my family manor were separated by miles of open green space. Neat, orderly neighborhoods of smaller dwellings marched row after row as far as the eye could see. It would take weeks to locate her by going door-to-door, and even if I found the right house, it was unlikely that the homeowners would admit she was there.

So, I made an educated guess and cut across the park toward the wealthiest neighborhood. I figured I was on the right track when the bracelet's lights began pulsing faster. Just to be sure, I switched direction. The pulsing stopped. The miniature light show resumed when I returned to my original course. I did a subtle fist pump and hurried on.

The bracelet led me to a gleaming white mansion surrounded by lush gardens, well-manicured lawns, and a polished marble wall topped with sparkling shards of glass. Unfortunately, it had a guard shack outside the massive iron gates, so climbing over that wall was out of the question. So was sneaking around to search for another way in, because, as I stood there thinking, the two guards spotted me. They were old acquaintances of mine, police elves Wildflower and Sunspot. And by acquaintances, I mean not friends.

Why were police patrolling this mansion? I wondered. Then I saw their rather plain uniforms and skinny billy clubs. They weren't cops anymore, but private security guards. After the last time I'd seen Sunspot and Wildflower, when my father had unleashed a herd of wild nøkks on them, they must have lost their badges. It was worth coming to Alfheim again just to see that.

I took the direct approach and walked up to the gate as if I had every right to be there. The guards' eyes widened with recognition and, I noted with satisfaction, a hint of fear. Sunspot darted into the guard shack. Wildflower, meanwhile, produced a bullhorn and put it to his mouth. I assumed he was yelling at me, but since his lips were covered, I couldn't tell what he was saying. And yes, he knew I was hearing-impaired. The fact that he used a bullhorn to communicate with a deaf person should tell you something about him.

Without breaking stride, I pulled *gebo*, the rune for *gift*, from my bag and lobbed it at Wildflower. He flinched as the stone bounced off his forehead. Then he blinked, straightened, and offered me the bullhorn.

I tucked the horn under my arm, touching my fingertips to my chin and signing *Thank you* as I walked past him to the gate. Sunspot remained in the guard shack, probably quaking in his rent-a-cop shoes. I pressed a *lagaz* rune against the lock. I must have put a little extra magical oomph into it, for the entire wrought-iron gate, not just the lock, lique-fied into a puddle of molten metal.

Whoops. My bad.

Halfway to the mansion, I reached for my dagaz rune. I planned to amplify my ASL-to-speech magic with the bull-horn and pretend to be a giant who had come to collect his long-lost Inge.

That plan fell apart when the ground began shaking. T.J.'s curse word flashed through my mind when I looked behind me and saw the cause of the tremors.

Sunspot must have called for backup. It was a huge, hideous troll. (How such an unattractive creature had been allowed, much less employed, in Alfheim, I don't know.) Protective sun-gear covered every inch of him and bore the same security-company logo. Even under his dingy white jumpsuit I could tell he had a massive chest and equally muscular legs, and I could see his yellow teeth and blood-shot eyes through the tinted plastic shield that hung down from his hood, covering his face. His thick gloved fingers flexed as if they itched to encircle and squeeze my neck.

The troll charged me like an angry rhino. A rather slow angry rhino, but still.

I dropped the bullhorn and scrabbled in my rune bag for the *algiz* protection stone. Backpedaling wildly, I hurled it at the troll's massive work boots. A shimmering energy shield sprang up. The troll bounced off it like a bumper car

ODIN

BLITZEN

HEARTHSTONE

SAMIRAH

T.J.

Mallory

HALFBORN

ALEX

and landed on his fleshy butt. The ground shuddered so violently I almost fell.

He didn't stay down long. With a roar so powerful I felt the sound vibrations, he punched his fist through the shield and came at me again.

I hit him with everything I had. *Isa*, the ice rune, slowed him down by turning the mansion's brick walkway into a skating rink. He stomped his boot, shattering both the ice and the bricks underneath. I tossed the *uruz* symbol above his head and dropped a very surprised ox on top of him. He flicked the animal off like a piece of lint and sent it flying, legs akimbo, into a nearby pond. Using my *hagalaz* stone, I pummeled him with grapefruit-size hail; then I blowtorched him with flames I summoned with my *kenaz* rune. But he still kept coming.

After using so many runes, I was nearing exhaustion. I darted around a corner of the house and hid in a nearby rosebush to catch my breath. Thorny yet secure, it gave me time to search my memory for a troll's weakness.

But I came up empty. As I crouched in the bush, waiting for the troll to kill me, the names my father used to call me echoed in my mind. *Worthless. Disgrace. Stupid.*

I was in danger of falling into a shame spiral when it hit me. *Names.* The best weapon against a troll is to learn its true name. Like a password, speaking the name out loud unlocks the way past the troll's natural defenses—its thick hide, its thicker skull, its bad breath.

Okay, I thought. *Now how do I get him to tell me his name?* Asking wouldn't work. Even if he understood ASL, I doubted he'd be stupid enough to answer my question. Then I remembered where I was—not the rosebush, but Alfheim.

Elves liked to feel superior to others—a skill my father had honed to a sharp, cutting edge. Perhaps a troll who lived here would, too. If I could get him to brag about himself, he might let his name slip.

I touched Inge's band for courage and emerged from the bush. The troll thundered over, arms outstretched and gloved fingers reaching for my neck. I flung up my hands in surrender. My heart hammered two beats before he lowered his meaty paws.

"What trickery is this?" he roared.

I feigned confusion, pointed to my ears, and shook my head.

The troll sneered. "Oh yes. The deaf elf who can do magic. I've heard of you. Mr. Alderman's brat, right?"

Through lip-reading and some guesswork, I got the gist of what he said, but I wrinkled my brow as if utterly baffled.

The troll circled me, still suspicious. His eyes darted to my rune bag. With a surprisingly quick move, he snatched it from my hands. "Ha! Now you're deaf *and* powerless!" Smirking, he dangled the bag just out of my reach.

I cowered appropriately but kept watching his lips.

JOTUNHEIM

"Oh yeah!" He tucked the bag into his belt. "What has two thumbs and just defeated the mighty Hearthstone?" He pointed his thumbs at himself. "This troll! And now this troll is going to have some fun."

He rearranged his expression to one of sympathy and bent forward, hands on knees, to look me in the eye. "I'm going to pretend to have second thoughts about killing you. First I'll gain your trust." He plucked a rose and held it out to me encouragingly.

I faked a look of growing hope and took it.

The troll smiled and patted me on the head. "Isn't that nice? What's even nicer is how I'm going kill you." He mimed opening a screw-top bottle and guzzling its contents. "I'll twist your head off your neck, then drink down all your blood. Yum, yum." He smacked his lips and offered me a sip from the pretend bottle.

Smiling hesitantly, I accepted and mimed taking a swig. On the inside, though, I was dying. Pretending to drink your own blood from your decapitated body has that effect.

"And you know what I'll do after that?" the troll continued. "I'll mount your head on a stick and fasten it to my vest so everyone will know that I, Siersgrunnr the Magnificent, bested the famous magic-wielding deaf elf!"

I almost gave myself away then, and not just because the troll had let his name slip. Roughly translated, *Siersgrunnr* means Cheesebutt. You try lip-reading that and not laughing.

Instead, I shoved my hand in my pocket and clasped the dagaz rune. With the other, I pointed to myself and then at the open gate. *I can go?*

"You want to leave? Oh, sure, sure. I don't mind killing you when your back is turned." He made a shooing motion to hurry me along.

Heart pounding, I walked a few paces toward the exit. I had no intention of leaving. I just wanted to move closer to the bullhorn.

The dagaz rune was heating up in my palm. It was now or never. I turned back to face the troll. Widening my eyes, I pointed at something over his shoulder. Oldest trick in the book—and he fell for it.

In one fluid sequence, I grabbed the bullhorn, hit the ON button, tossed dagaz into the air, and spelled out the troll's name in rapid-fire ASL.

"Siersgrunnr!"

Cheesebutt whirled around, his face contorting in sudden fear. He knew he was weaker now that his name had been spoken. "Who—who said that?"

I dropped the bullhorn and jerked two thumbs at myself. Then I darted forward and grabbed my rune bag. The *tiwaz* stone—the rune of Tyr, the god of war—practically leaped into my fingers. I used it to transform the rose into a thorn-spiked club. One swing took him out at the knees. A second knocked him unconscious.

Once they realized they couldn't hide behind Cheesebutt any longer, Wildflower and Sunspot raced up from the guard shack, their billy clubs at the ready. But the double threat of my rune bag and spiked club sent them running right back to the gate again—and into the hills beyond.

My bracelet sparkled.

Inge.

I mounted the house's front steps and banged on the door with the thorn club.

Someone inside must have seen everything. The door opened, Inge was shoved out, and then it slammed shut again. Inge leaped into my arms.

After a moment, I pulled back and signed, *Are you okay?*

She nodded and signed back, *You were brilliant. They were terrified. They—*

She suddenly froze and stared past me in shock. Tremors shook the ground. Had the troll awakened? I spun and thrust Inge behind me.

Then I relaxed. The troll was still lying where I'd left him. The tremors were from a different, but equally disturbing source: Thor.

"Hello, Mr. Elf, Ms. Hulder!" he called as he jogged by.

Hi, Thor, I signed. *Nice shorts.*

Thor stopped and pointed at his earbuds. "Sorry, I'm listening to rock! Maybe you should use the bullhorn."

Or I could just sign louder.

"Add in bicep curls for a full-body workout?" Thor hefted his hammer, Mjolnir. "A worthwhile suggestion, Mr. Elf! Well, good-bye!"

Thor thundered off.

Usually, I'd leave Alfheim just as quickly. This time, though, I didn't mind staying a bit longer. Maybe it was the success of the dagaz magic or defeating a troll single-handedly.

But I suspect Inge's smiling face had something to do with it.

My Eighth-Grade Physics Actually Comes in Handy

BY SAMIRAH AL-ABBAS

"I ASSUME you know why I summoned you here, Samirah." Odin sat back in his desk chair and regarded me expectantly.

I willed myself not to squirm. "Um, if it's about how I butt-dialed you during that einherji acquisition just now, I can explain. See, she was thrashing a lot, and my phone was in my back pocket and—"

Odin silenced me with a raised hand. "I admit that overhearing your struggle was . . . unsettling. Such an excessive amount of grunting and cursing. It reminded me of my survival-training seminar with Bear Grylls. Who is not, incidentally, an actual bear. But I digress." He leaned forward over his desk. "I have a new job for you."

A thrill shot up my spine. Since becoming Odin's

Valkyrie in charge of special assignments, I'd gone on several dangerous missions. No doubt this next one would prove just as challenging.

"Whatever it is, Lord Odin," I replied fervently, "I'm your Valkyrie."

He nodded with satisfaction. "Excellent." He opened a folder and slid a grainy photograph across the desk to me. "Tell me, what do you make of that?"

I studied the image carefully. "It's an egg."

He rolled his hand, encouraging me to continue.

"A red egg. In a nest."

"Exactly. But not just any egg." He picked up a remote and pushed a button. A video screen descended from the spear-enhanced ceiling and locked into place. He pushed another button. Images of wolves, giants, gods, and weapons flashed across the screen. Then a title: *The Signs of Ragnarok: Doomed if You Know Them, Doomed if You Don't.*

I groaned inwardly. I'd sat through Odin's instructional video when I first became a Valkyrie. I saw it a second time after I helped re-shackle the dreaded killer Fenris Wolf on Lyngvi, the Isle of Heather. Then once more after I'd inadvertently aided my father Loki, a vile trickster, to escape his imprisonment. And after Loki was recaptured? Yep—got to see it again.

To my immense relief, Odin fast-forwarded past the early warning signs: the death of his beloved son Balder, the three years of endless snow and ice known as Fimbulwinter, and the wolves who swallow the sun and the moon. He paused on a shot of three roosters.

"According to all sources, one sign of Ragnarok is the crowing of these roosters." He circled each bird with a laser pointer as he identified it. "Gullinkambi, who will hatch right here in Asgard. Fialar, whose egg resides in Jotunheim. And Nameless, the future foul fowl of Helheim."

I raised my hand tentatively. "Excuse me, sir, just to clarify—the rooster's name is Nameless?"

"It has no name, so I named it Nameless."

"Oh."

Odin stood up and paced the room. "In a recent scan of the Nine Worlds, I confirmed that Gullinkambi and Nameless are still in egg form, which is good—*very* good—because they are unlikely to herald Ragnarok while in their shells." His piercing blue eye flicked over to me. "It's the third egg that has me concerned."

I picked up the photo. "The egg of Fialar. In Jotunheim."

"That photo was taken three months ago by—well, you don't need to know that. But now the earth giants have blocked my view of the nest with their distortion magic. I suspect they are hiding something from me. That's where you come in."

My heart leaped with excitement. Odin was sending me to fight the jotuns in Jotunheim! I jumped up and summoned my spear of light. It blazed with anticipation. "I won't let you down, sir! I'll take care of those giants *and* their wretched sorcery!"

"Ah. No." Odin handed me a Valkyrie Vision body cam. "I need you to take a new photo of the egg. So I can see if it is beginning to hatch."

My spear dimmed. "Oh."

He raised an eyebrow. "It's an important job. Likely fraught with danger."

"Oh, sure," I agreed. "Snapping a pic of an egg in a nest would be . . . obviously. I'll be on my way, then."

"Take a mount if you wish. But you will need to be discreet. I don't want the giants to know you were ever there. And this warning, Samirah: Your magic hijab will be of no use in Jotunheim. On their own turf, giants can see through that kind of magic."

My hijab has the ability to camouflage me and one other person. Being hidden from enemies had come in handy in the past. Not this time, though, it seemed.

I nodded to show my understanding, then departed with the photo and body cam.

Minutes later, I was winging over the earth giants' land on a horse made of mist. I'd been to parts of Jotunheim before and used familiar landmarks, like the crumbled ruins where a particularly nasty family of giants once lived, to get my bearings. When I didn't see any eggs or nests in that zone, I expanded my search parameters.

Finally, I saw the nest perched on a hilltop surrounded by a forest. It matched the photo Odin had shown me—a thatch-work of leaves, sticks, grass, and what I really hoped wasn't human hair—but was much bigger in person, about the size of an aboveground swimming pool. The bowl of the nest was deep. If the egg was inside, I couldn't see it. I nudged the horse downward and dismounted in a distant clearing. The horse took one look at the trees and bolted back into the sky.

I couldn't blame her. The trees were unbelievably creepy—pitch-black and gnarled, with thick ropy vines twisting throughout their branches. As I walked past one loop of vine swinging in the wind, I recalled the forest's name from an old picture book about Jotunheim: Gallows-wood. I shuddered and kept walking to the hill.

Get a grip, Sam, I scolded myself. *They're just–* Oh, *Helheim,* I cursed, dropping into a crouch.

Coming over the far side of the hill was a giant. He was skyscraper tall. Muscles bulged beneath his dark shirt and pants. His receding salt-and-pepper hair was shorn tight to his skull. Interestingly, he had a golden harp dangling from his belt instead of a weapon.

I crossed my fingers and hoped that he was just passing through. But he settled on the nest like a mother hen, carefully tucking the harp in next to him.

"Play!" he commanded. The harp immediately plucked out a tune. The giant cleared his throat and sang along.

"I am Eggther,
Protector of the egg.
If you dare come near me,
I will break your leg."

My mouth turned dry. Had the giant seen me?

"Gouge out both your eyes
And punch you in the throat.
Squeeze you dry into a cup
To make a blood-beer float."

Despite the horrific lyrics, I relaxed. The "you" in Eggther's song didn't seem specific to me. I hoped.

Still, I was in a quandary. So long as the minstrel of Gallows-wood sat on the egg, I couldn't snap my photo. With Eggther's rousing refrain ringing in my ears—*Bash, maim, squish, splat / Pound and kick until you're flat*—I backtracked silently into the woods to consider my options. One: I could return to Valhalla and explain to Odin why I'd failed. Two: I could ask Eggther to pose for a photo with the egg. Three: I could try bashing Eggther before he bashed me.

I was leaning toward Option Two when Eggther stopped singing and started snoring. I risked a peek. He was fast asleep, chin on his chest and a line of drool dribbling from his mouth. Unfortunately, he was still sitting on the egg. That ruled out Option Three, for while I could now easily bash him, I wouldn't have a prayer of moving his body off the nest. I'm strong, but not that strong.

Then my gaze landed on the harp. Seeing it reminded me of an old fairy tale, "Jack and the Beanstalk." The giant in that story had a self-playing golden harp, too. When Jack stole the harp, it alerted the giant by playing loudly. (I always hated the harp for that.) I was willing to bet Eggther's harp would do the same.

I formed a plan. Using the vines, I'd sneak up, rope the harp, and fly off with it. My nebulous horse would have been ideal for this part, but I can fly on my own in short bursts. The harp would sing out—hopefully—the giant would wake up and chase after it—probably—and I'd drop the harp, circle back, snap the egg pic, and hightail it back to Asgard.

Amazingly, everything went according to plan—right up until it didn't. The problem? Golden harps are heavy. Like, really, *really* heavy. When I pulled the rope to lift it, it wouldn't budge. Luckily, it didn't play, either, though I detected a bit of sleepy humming. I took that as a good sign that if—when—I dislodged it, it would sing out an alarm.

I retreated back to Gallows-wood to ponder the problem.

You know how you think you'll never use math and science outside of school? Well, an eighth-grade physics lesson about moving heavy objects with a rope saved the day. Basically, a heavy object can be shifted by attaching one end of a rope to the object, the other to a fixed, immovable object, and then pulling on the rope's center point.

One end of my vine rope was already looped around the harp. I tied the other around a stout tree at the bottom of the hill. Then I wrapped my hijab around my waist like a harness, tied it to the rope's midpoint, and backpedaled until the rope formed a taut V. According to physics, if I pulled hard enough, the harp would move.

"Here goes nothing," I muttered.

I faced the inside of the V so I could keep an eye on the harp and the giant. Then I threw myself back into the harness like the anchor on a tug-of-war team. My legs pushed against the earth, muscles straining.

The harp rocked slightly, made an ominous thrumming sound, and then settled back into place.

Cursing, I tried again. My foot slipped and I fell. Rubbing my tailbone, I gave myself a quick pep talk.

Come on, al-Abbas! You can do this! You can—

I paused in mid-pep. Something was coming around the hill. Something big and hairy and fast. Something in butt-hugging leather shorts. And it was coming right toward me.

"Thor!" I yelled frantically. "Stop! Or at least detour!"

He didn't hear me. I scrabbled frantically at the knot in my hijab. It came loose a split second before Thor barreled up. In one motion I put the hijab back over my head and dove to one side. His foot caught the rope, but he didn't break stride.

Twang!

The rope went taut, popping the tree out of the ground

like a cork from a champagne bottle. The harp burst out of the nest at the same time.

"Well, that worked," I said.

As I'd hoped, the harp's strings began plucking out a frantic alarm. The volume increased as it bounced along the ground behind Thor and left Eggther behind. Eggther woke up.

"Hey!" he yelled. "That's mine!" He jumped up and gave chase.

I flew into the air to make sure the giant stayed focused on the thunder god instead of me. From my vantage point, I was treated to a truly bizarre sight: Thor puffing along, the tree and the harp bouncing behind him, Eggther trying to snatch the instrument in the air while bellowing threats. If you'd like to see it for yourself, feel free to take a look at the Valkyrie Vision video I "accidentally" shot.

With Eggther safely out of the way, I checked on the egg. Not a crack anywhere on its bright red shell. I was no bird expert, but I figured that meant Fialar wasn't hatching anytime soon. I was tempted to fly back to Asgard with it so we could keep a close watch on the future rooster of doom.

But I knew it wouldn't make a difference. Fialar would hatch in Jotunheim as foretold, and it would crow someday, and Ragnarok would come.

So, I did what I was sent to do.

"Say cheese!"

HELHEIM

Nice Doggy

BY THOMAS "T.J." JEFFERSON JR.

"I'VE SAID it before, and I'll say it again." I flumped back onto the battered sofa of floor nineteen's lounge and patted my stomach. "Santarpio's pizza is worth sneaking out for."

I reached for another slice.

"Uh-uh. You've had plenty." Mallory dropped the pizza box lid over the remains and stood up. "I'm taking this to Halfborn. He's been holed up in his room all day doing who knows what. Probably forgot to eat, the big dumbo. Catch you later."

I gave her a lazy wave, then stretched out on the sofa with a sigh of contentment, my trusty rifle and bone-steel bayonet by my side. The warmth from the fire flickering in the hearth enveloped me like a soft blanket. My eyelids grew heavy. I dozed off and, as my mother used to say, fell into dreamland.

At least, that's where I thought I'd fallen. But the desolate rocky terrain, the bone-chilling dampness, the low moaning carried by the wind—they seemed too real to be just a dream. Real, and frightening. Somehow I had entered another world. I'd heard that eating pizza before bedtime can cause nightmares, but I didn't think it could transport a person.

Then I heard a yell.

"Coming through!"

I spun to see Thor charging toward me like a runaway locomotive. Arms pumping and leather Daisy Duke shorts riding up where the sun don't shine—dream or no, I wasn't stupid enough to stand in the way of *that*. I leaped back as he blew past me, and then scrambled away even farther to avoid being clubbed by something bouncing along behind him. A tree—and was that a *harp?*—on a long rope attached to his ankle, near as I could make out.

"Well," I murmured, "that just happened."

I watched as Thor zigzagged through a hardscrabble landscape at the base of a jagged outcropping. Suddenly, there was a sharp bark. An enormous hound emerged from a cliff-top cave, far above Thor. As big as a Mack truck, with black fur dotted with red splotches, the dog stared down at the oblivious god and his toys-on-a-rope, panting with an openmouthed dog-smile on its face. It barked again—joyfully, I thought—then chased after Thor and the tree. Flecks of red dripped off its body as it picked its way down the steep incline.

I suddenly realized what the red splotches were: *blood*. The hound's muzzle, fur, and paws were stained with it.

Recognition clicked in my brain as first Thor and then the hound disappeared in the distance. I stumbled back onto the nearest boulder and sat down hard.

"Garm," I said aloud to myself. "The guardian dog of Helheim. And—"

"Your father's killer."

A woman spoke close to my ear. I whirled around. A kaleidoscope of colors spun and twisted before my eyes. When it cleared, I was no longer standing in a barren moonscape but in a grand hall next to a throne made out of charred logs. Gray drapes hung from the ceiling to the polished black marble floor. Grotesque bronze statues, the bodies contorted in postures of agony, sorrow, and terror, lined one wall. More statues lined the opposite wall, but these were rendered to express joy, love, and humor. I chose to look at that side.

A figure in a hooded ermine cloak appeared on the throne. The woman's voice spoke again. "You're not dreaming, einherji, but having a vision. You're here in mind, not in body, and seeing recent events I've chosen for you to see." She pushed back the hood and smiled.

"Oh," I said. "Hel."

I'd seen my share of horrors during the War Between the States. Rotting corpses torn apart by scavenger birds. Legless soldiers staring dead-eyed at the sky. Bloated, water-logged remains floating in stagnant ponds.

The right half of Hel's face beat them all. Blackened teeth, cataract-filmed eye, pocked skull, open ear hole. Not even the beauty of her left side—and it was stop-you-dead-in-your-tracks beautiful—could offset the horror of her ghoulish half.

She snapped her skeletal fingers. Double doors at the far end of the hall blew open. Two demons dragged a ghostly woman in chains before the throne and forced her to kneel. The woman lifted her head and glared daggers at Hel.

I sucked in a sharp breath.

The woman was my mother—my sweet mother, who sang me to sleep and smelled like warm corn bread and butter. I hadn't seen her for more than a hundred years.

I choked back a sob. *"Mom."* My mother's gaze didn't waver from Hel, and I remembered that my body was back on the hotel couch. To see her after so long, and for her not to see or hear me . . . it just about broke my heart.

Hel noted my reaction and smiled. "Oh, good. You still have feelings for her."

"Feelings for who?" my mother demanded. "Who are you talking to?"

Hel ignored her. "So you won't want her to suffer," she said to me.

I stared at Hel with loathing. "Of course I don't!"

"Who is going to suffer?" my mother cried.

"Then come to me, einherji," Hel said. "In the flesh. I have a job that only a child of Tyr can do. Oh, and don't tell a soul . . . or she will pay."

Hel inclined her head. The demons pulled the chains in opposite directions. My mother's body spasmed in pain. But her eyes never left Hel's face, and she didn't cry out.

I did.

I woke up on the sofa drenched in sweat, with the scream still in my throat and the vision of my mother suffering in my mind's eye.

"Hang on, Mom. I'm coming!"

I grabbed my rifle and bayonet, ran down the hallway, and banged on Alex's door. "I need tree access!" I bellowed. When Alex opened the door, I pushed past and shinnied up the trunk of the World Tree, searching for a branch to take me to Helheim.

YARK!

Ratatosk, the evil giant squirrel, was lying in wait. It let out a stream of insults that pummeled me like body blows to the psyche.

You couldn't help her when you were alive. You won't save her now that you're dead. Your friends mock you for hiding behind that ridiculous bayonet. They think you're stupid. Weak. Brainless.

I kept moving despite the barrage, but my thoughts sank deeper and deeper into a black pit of despair.

Suddenly, the insults ceased. I tumbled through an opening in a branch into Hel's grand hall—for real this time. Hel was on her throne, but my mother and the demons were nowhere to be seen.

"I see you discovered the key: the despair that Ratatosk induces helps one gain access to my world," the goddess said. "Now kneel before me, einherji."

I hesitated, then did as the goddess of the dishonorable dead commanded. For my mother's sake.

She studied me. "You are aware that my hellhound, Garm, will devour your father, Tyr, when Ragnarok is unleashed?"

I nodded.

"As Tyr's spawn, you have his blood in your veins."

I nodded again, wondering where this was going.

"Well. Garm has run off," she told me. "You, son of Tyr, are the only one who can find him. Or rather"—she treated me to a ghastly smile—"he will find *you*."

"I don't follow."

"Why, it's very simple. My hellhound will smell the blood of Tyr and come running."

I clutched my rifle more tightly. "So basically, you're using me as bait."

"More like a moving target," Hel amended.

"Why me?" I dared to ask. "Why not just, I don't know, poof Garm back to his cave yourself? Or send your demons to retrieve him?"

"Garm can be . . . elusive," she said evasively. "He's run

off before, and past attempts to bring him home with magic and demons have failed."

I was going to suggest she use a hellhound whistle, but I thought better of it. "If you don't mind my asking, why not just let him stay lost?"

Hel's expression darkened. "And risk word getting out that my dog is beyond my control? No. There is only one solution. You must lure him back to his cave."

I scowled. "Let me guess. If I refuse, you torture my mother. If I tell anyone Garm didn't come when you called, you torture my mother."

"Oh yes. And Thomas . . . T.J. . . . if you think killing Garm will stop the hound from killing your father, think again. You cannot stop destiny. Now, away you go!"

The double doors blew open. I shouldered my rifle and set off to search for a lost dog in the land of the dishonorable dead.

One thing my earlier vision failed to reveal? The doomed residents of Helheim. As I crossed the landscape, their ghostly forms swirled and brushed up against me, as if sensing I didn't belong in their afterlife. Most drifted off when I ignored them. But one ghost refused to leave me alone. It poked me repeatedly with something prickly.

"Listen, pal," I snapped, turning to confront him, "I don't know what your deal is, but . . ."

My voice died when I saw who'd been irritating me: the god Balder. The son of Odin and Frigg, Balder had been greatly beloved and, supposedly, invulnerable to all forms of attack. But he had one weakness: mistletoe. Loki had tricked Balder's blind brother, Hod, into killing Balder with a mistletoe arrow—the same arrow he was now jabbing me with.

"Uh, hi," I said. "Anytime you want to stop doing that is fine by me."

Balder smiled, and I suddenly understood why the worlds had mourned his death. Young and handsome, with a mop of dark brown hair, sparkling blue eyes, and killer dimples on either side of his impish smile, Balder radiated warmth and good humor. Being near him made me feel happy. Plain and simple as that.

"Hi! You're Tyr's kid, right?"

I shouldn't have been startled that he could speak—after all, I'm dead too and I can talk just fine—but I near about jumped out of my skin when he did.

"Sorry about the poking," Balder went on. "We don't get many full-bodied visitors down here. That's why I followed you. But when you didn't react right away, I wasn't sure you were real."

I rubbed my sore arm. "I'm real."

"I'm glad," Balder said with another warm smile. "I always admired Tyr. Not because he let Fenris Wolf chomp off his hand while tying up that demon dog, but for how he handled himself with Odin and Thor."

I nodded to show my understanding. Long, long, ago,

Tyr had been the chief god of war. Over time, though, Odin and Thor rose in popularity and edged him out. My dad could have mounted an attack to regain his position, but he recognized the turmoil that civil war would have caused. So instead he stepped back and let Odin and Thor remain in power.

"Plus," Balder added, "Tyr was one of the few gods who didn't throw things at me to test my invulnerability. I always appreciated that."

"Enough to save him from being devoured by Garm?" I asked hopefully.

Balder shook his head. "I can't stop Garm from killing your father any more than I could stop this mistletoe arrow from killing me."

"If you don't mind my asking, why do you still have that thing?"

Balder pulled a face. "I tried to get rid of the arrow when I first got here. Burned it, buried it, crushed it with a rock, lost it accidentally on purpose. Nothing worked. It always reappeared back here." He pointed to his chest. "Now I just carry it around. In my hand," he added for clarity. "It gets in the way otherwise."

"Mm, I can see how it would. And did the poison in the mistletoe ever make you sick?"

He looked at me with surprise. "Poison?"

"Well, yeah," I said, equally surprised that he didn't know. "Mistletoe is poisonous. There was this old hound dog that used to hang around my regiment. One day it ate some mistletoe and—" I broke off.

"And what?" Balder asked anxiously. "The dog didn't die, did it? I hate stories where the dog dies!"

"No, but . . ." My mind was whirling. "It started walking funny and drooling and throwing up." I turned to him. "Balder, I need your help."

I told him about Garm, Thor, and my quest to find Hel's dog and save my mother from torture.

Balder shook his head. "I'm sorry, son of Tyr. I want to help you, but Hel would never permit me to intervene."

"Not you. That." I pointed to his arrow. "If Garm eats it, it might stop him. Not kill him," I added quickly, "just incapacitate him."

"It's true Garm wouldn't be killed. Not here, in Hel's realm. But if he ingests the mistletoe," Balder said, "maybe he won't feel like ingesting you!"

"Bonus," I agreed.

A loud baying cut through the stillness. A second later, Garm bounded over a hilltop. He sniffed the air and swiveled his massive head in my direction. The hound of Helheim had smelled me out.

I grabbed Balder's arrow. "You wouldn't happen to have a bow on you, by any chance?"

"Sorry. Fresh out."

"Right. Special delivery it is, then." I gripped my rifle in one hand and the arrow in the other. "Wish me luck!"

"I can't! Hel wouldn't approve!"

I didn't wait for Garm to come to me any more than I'd waited for Johnny Reb back in the war. Yelling at the top of my lungs, I ran full force at the hellhound.

Garm snarled and pounced. His bloodstained jaws opened wide, giving me an up close and personal view of his doggy uvula. I darted toward him, intending to shove the mistletoe into his mouth. His jaws snapped shut before I could, nearly taking off my hand when they did.

Then my battle training at Hotel Valhalla kicked into high gear. I spun away before he could take another bite, then jabbed my bayonet into his backside. He yelped loud enough to wake the dead. I pulled my bone-steel bayonet free and raced off in search of cover while he whirled in a circle, trying to lick his wound.

I spotted a ditch and jumped in. Flattening myself against the side, I plotted my next attack. I'd gotten as far as *avoid the snapping jaws* when I was enveloped in a blast of hot breath. I looked up to find Garm panting down at me, his drool-slick tongue hanging like a thick, wet blanket.

"Gross!" I rolled away just as that tongue tried to lap me up. Springing to my feet, I scrambled out of the trench and took a running leap onto Garm's neck—and immediately slipped on his blood-soaked fur and slid down the other side. I nicked him with the arrow, though, which must have been irritating, for he plunked down on his butt and vigorously scratched at his neck with his back paw.

Meanwhile, I ran across the field and hid behind a massive two-story-tall boulder, where I took stock of my situation. The straight-on attack had failed. Hiding in the ditch had been nearly fatal. So maybe it was time to take the high ground.

"Right," I growled. "This ends now."

One side of the boulder offered decent hand- and footholds. Silently thanking Hotel Valhalla for installing a climbing wall, I slung my rifle over my shoulder, stuck the arrow through my belt, and scaled my way to the top.

"Hey, you overgrown puggle," I bellowed from my perch, "how about a nice tasty Tyr-flavored treat? Yeah? You want a piece of me?"

Garm stopped scratching and started snarling. He padded over and circled the boulder. He tried to scramble up, but his paws couldn't find purchase.

"Looks like you're going hungry tonight!" I taunted.

Garm growled with frustration. Then, eyes locked on me, he backed away and got into a crouch.

I crouched too, slipping the arrow from my belt as I did. Then I waited.

Not for very long. With a loud howl, Garm charged. When he reached the boulder, he pounced. His muscular back legs sent him flying up the side straight at me, paws reaching out and mouth yawning wide.

At the last possible second, I stepped to the side. Then, with a cry of fury, I jammed the arrow straight down his gullet, yanking my hand free just before his teeth crushed it. My attack threw him off-balance, and he landed with a flop on top of the boulder. While he scrabbled to get his footing, I leaped to the ground and ran like Helheim back to where I'd first seen him: the rocky outcrop I assumed was his cave.

At first, Garm chased me at top speed. I stayed one step ahead with a combination of wily zigzagging maneuvers I'd perfected over centuries of combat on Valhalla's battlefield. That, and sheer dumb luck.

But slowly, the hellhound fell behind. I risked a look back. Garm's mouth foamed as the mistletoe's poison went to work. By the time we reached his cave, he was a wobbling, whimpering mess. I kind of felt bad for him.

All sympathy vanished when he threw up. Thankfully, it didn't splash on me, but the smell was really, really disgusting. Garm tottered into his cave, fell onto his doggy bed of crushed bones, and began snoring.

Balder wandered in then. Ignoring the puke, he pried open the dog's jaws, waded into its throat, and retrieved his arrow. "So I can wash it off before I wake up with it sticking out of my chest," he explained.

He was about to say something else. But whatever it was, I didn't hear it, because Hel chose that moment to send me back to Valhalla. I had no idea whether she would keep her promise to spare my mother.

I got my answer that night. The goddess of death visited

me in a dream. "A job well done, son of Tyr," she said. "Your mother is safe. I may even grant you permission to visit her from time to time."

Warring emotions bubbled up in my gut then—anger at how my mother had been treated, and elation that one day I might get to see her again. Elation won out.

"I look forward to that," I said. "And I'm glad your dog is back home, even though he's destined to kill my dad. But right now, do me a favor." I rolled over and pulled up the covers. "Go to Helheim."

NIFLHEIM

So's Your Face!

BY MALLORY KEEN

"DRAGON SCALES."

Standing in the floor nineteen hallway, half-empty pizza box in hand, I glared at Halfborn Gunderson. He'd opened his door just a crack. "You're seriously telling me you're traveling to Vanaheim to get dragon scales?" I asked. "Straight off a dragon, no less?"

"It's for a little project I'm working on." The shirtless berserker avoided my eyes. Coward.

I tried to push my way in, but my on-again, off-again boyfriend set his massive foot against the slightly ajar door, making our relationship dangerously close to off again.

"That's the way you want to play it? Fine." I snatched a

slice of pizza from the box, slapped him in the chest with it, and stormed off.

"Mallory! Wait!"

When I didn't stop, Halfborn swore a blue streak and slammed his door. Maybe he was looking for his room key, planning to follow. Well, I didn't want to see him or his pizza-stained chest anymore. So I bypassed my room, yanked open a random door, and stalked through, slamming it behind me.

Then I literally froze.

"Oh, Fimbulwinter."

Hotel Valhalla has countless unmarked doors. Most are shortcuts to other areas of the hotel. A few lead to other worlds. Just my luck, I'd exited right into Niflheim, the land of endless sleet and ice, and plenty of frost giants. Even luckier, a blizzard was raging around me. Cursing, I dug a small square of fabric out of my pocket. Handmade by Blitzen, it unfolded into a thick hooded parka infused with kenaz (fire) magic, courtesy of Hearthstone. Ever since I'd journeyed to Niflheim to help stop Loki—long story—I made sure to carry it with me. Nestled in its warm embrace, I turned back and groped for the doorknob.

There wasn't one. No door, either. Instead, I found myself peering at a mile-high wall of solid ice.

"A glacier? You have *got* to be kidding me."

I scrubbed a circle in the frost and peered into the glacier to see . . . more ice. I pounded on the slab. Attacked it with my twin daggers. Kicked it and screamed at it. I worked up a good sweat, but if Hotel Valhalla was somewhere on the other side, I wasn't getting back in the way I came out.

I sheathed my daggers, put a hand on the glacier, and began walking, trailing my fingers on the icy wall to feel for a door, a knob, a window—something. Then the wall ended and my frozen fingers plunged into a massive snowdrift.

Growling with frustration, I shoved my hands in my pockets and turned back. The glacier was the only connection I had to the hotel, and I didn't want to lose sight of it. I'd only gone a few steps when I heard a muffled thudding in the distance. I paused. The thudding grew louder and closer.

Frost giant.

The possibility struck me like a slushball in the face. I knew from past experience that some frost giants were friendly. They weren't the ones I was worried about.

A solitary figure loomed into view through the driving snow. My first thought was *How can he not be freezing in those short-shorts?* My second was *Jump!*

I leaped to one side as Thor pounded past.

"Hey! Wait!" I started after him, but immediately skidded to a halt. Thor was letting out farts like a sputtering engine. A cloud of noxious fumes enveloped me.

"Gods of Asgard!" I waved a hand in front of my face. "What crawled up inside him and died?"

Coughing, eyes smarting, I almost failed to recognize

the one plus of the situation. Ever hear the phrase *like a hot knife through butter?* Well, substitute *fart stream* for *knife* and *snow drifts* for *butter.* Thor's gas was melting a wide trail that made walking through Niflheim a hundred times easier. I figured he would eventually end up in Asgard, so I followed in his smelly wake.

Unfortunately, Thor was too fast for me to keep up. Then the blizzard filled in his trail, obliterating it completely. I swallowed my rising panic and pushed on through the stinging snow.

For a while, all I heard was the whine of the wind and my own heavy breathing. But then a new sound entered the mix. A gurgling, like water. I stopped, thinking. Water might mean a river or a stream. Maybe I could follow it out of Niflheim? With Thor's trail gone, it seemed like my best option. I detoured and headed toward the sound.

The air gradually warmed. I quickened my pace. The driving snow changed into fat, wet flakes that gave way to a thick gray mist. I took off my parka, folded it back into a square, and stuck it in my pocket.

The gurgling changed too, to a bubbling, like water coming to a boil. I paused. Good thing I did. The fog parted momentarily to reveal a vast steaming body of water directly ahead of me. A few more strides and I'd have stepped off a steep bank into its inky black depths.

What is this place? My mind sifted through my knowledge

of the Nine Worlds and came up with the answer. *It's Hvergelmir, the hot spring surrounding the roots of Yggdrasil! Yes!*

I did a little happy dance. If I could get to the tree's roots, I could climb Yggdrasil back to Asgard or some other, more hospitable world.

Peering through the mist, I could just make out the twisted and humped roots sticking out of the black water like the knees of cypress trees—only much, much bigger. I caught a quick glimpse of Yggdrasil's trunk stretching skyward from their midst before the steam shrouded it from my view.

So, my Niflheim exit was out there. Getting to it, however, presented some problems. I'm a decent swimmer, but I wasn't convinced I could make it across Hvergelmir without being boiled alive by the hot spring water. With my einherji power, I could have tried jumping the whole expanse. But the mist made it difficult to see where the water ended and the roots began. If I misjudged the distance, who knew where I might land.

There's got to be a way, I thought. I circled the pool. On the opposite side, I spotted an undulating root stretching to the shoreline like a long section of roller coaster. It was treacherously slick with humidity and green moss. But it was the only bridge I could see over the water.

Sweat beading down my face and hands feeling for purchase, I crawled across the root inch by inch. After what seemed an eternity, I reached the other side. I rolled off onto moist loamy earth. I picked my way through the outer roots and sat against one near Yggdrasil to catch my breath.

The root twitched. Gasping, I scrambled back. Nothing in my memory banks said Yggdrasil could move.

I looked closer at the root. It was brown and green, but unlike the other, mossy roots twisting around it, this root looked decidedly scaly. While my mind processed that fact, I heard a chewing sound. My heart sank.

It's not a root. It's Nidhogg's tail.

In my rush to get to Yggdrasil, I'd forgotten about Nidhogg, the dragon that lives at the World Tree's base. Nidhogg spends his days gnawing on the tree's roots and trading taunts with an eagle that nests in the treetops. Ratatosk, the gigantic insult squirrel, acts as go-between, delivering messages from roots to treetop and back again.

Now, I myself am a fan of the barbed word. Insults come in handy with an oafish lout like Halfborn. But to cast aspersions upon one another for millennia, the way the eagle, dragon, and squirrel do? I'd never let our relationship reach that level of dysfunction.

Nidhogg's green-and-brown body was coiled around the base of the tree. To climb out of Niflheim via Yggdrasil, I'd first have to climb over Nidhogg. That prospect did not thrill me, especially when I spied the claws on his powerful back legs. I moved to look for the dragon's head—*always know where the dangerous mouth parts are*, is my motto—and put my foot right into a pile of bones. *Crunch!* Apparently, Yggdrasil's roots weren't the only things Nidhogg gnawed on.

I unsheathed my daggers, expecting the dragon to attack at the sound. Instead, he muttered to himself.

"That eagle thinks he's all that. Well, my new insult will be so scathing he'll molt his feathers. Now all I have to do is think it up."

A gleam of hope sparked inside me. Nidhogg needed an insult? I had a million of them. Maybe we could cut a deal— one eagle-bashing zinger for safe passage up the tree. No guarantee Nidhogg wouldn't devour me on sight, of course, but it was the only plan I had, so I went for it.

I kicked a rib cage off my foot and swaggered around the tree as if I owned the place. "Hey there!"

Startled, Nidhogg stopped in mid-mutter. He stared at me, his huge yellow eyes blinking in confusion. Then, nostrils flaring dangerously, he let out a bellow that doubled as an impressive display of razor-sharp fangs.

My heart faltered, but I swallowed my fear and pressed on.

"Is that supposed to intimidate me?" I made a big show of rolling my eyes. "I've heard louder roars from Thor's butt."

Nidhogg flinched as if I'd whacked him on the nose with a rolled-up newspaper. "That wasn't very nice." He sounded so hurt I almost felt sorry for him.

Instead, I snorted with derision. "Buddy, I insult everyone." I waved my daggers. "See these? They're sharp, but not as sharp as my tongue." *Or your fangs,* I added to myself as the dragon loomed in closer to inspect my blades.

"Wow. Those *are* pointy." Nidhogg looked genuinely impressed. "Are your insults really sharper than that?"

"Mister, that question is so dumb it makes me think your brain is like Odin's left eye socket—completely empty."

Nidhogg winced. "Wow. That really, really hurt. But you're right, of course." He tapped a daggerlike claw against his skull. "My brain is empty. Of insults, anyway."

That was my opening. I sheathed my daggers and cocked my head to one side as if considering something. "You know, I have some powerful one-liners that never fail to infuriate. I'd be willing to share a few, but what's in it for me?"

Nidhogg scratched his belly. "Well, for starters, I won't eat you," he offered.

"Hmm. Tell you what. Let me climb up Yggdrasil when we're done, and you've got a deal."

Nidhogg stuck out a claw. I thought he was going to slice me to ribbons, but then I realized he wanted to shake on it. I did so, very carefully.

"Okay," I said, "now listen closely."

Nidhogg swept down and pressed his ear to my mouth.

"Not that closely."

"Sorry." He backed off.

"Right. Let's start with the four classic retorts: One: *I know you are, but what am I?* Two: *I'm rubber, you're glue—whatever you say bounces off me and sticks to you.* Three: *Takes one to know one.* And four: *So's your face!"*

Nidhogg's eyes widened with astonishment. "Those are *brilliant!*" His bellow blew my hair back. "Let's test them out."

I shrugged. "You are one ugly snake."

Nidhogg recoiled, the wounded expression back on his face.

"That was your cue to use one of the retorts," I explained.

His face cleared. "Oh yeah! Ha-ha!"

"Let's try again. You are one ugly snake."

"I know I am, but what are you?" He smiled with delight.

I am never getting out of here, I thought. Out loud, I said, "Let's go over that wording again."

After a few more sample rounds, Nidhogg got the hang of it. By then I was enjoying myself, so I threw in some simple bird-themed taunts for him to use against the eagle: *You're so loony, cuckoos think you're crazy!*, *No birds of a feather would want to flock together with you!*, and *I heard you taste like chicken!*

In retrospect, that last one might have been a mistake. When Nidhogg heard it, his stomach growled. He gave me a sideways, hungry look. "So, um, want to stay for dinner?"

I casually sidled away from his mouth region. "Much as I'd love to, I should get back to Valhalla. Okay if I climb up over your coils now?"

"I'm rubber, you're glue!"

I took that as consent.

I'd never been happier to feel Yggdrasil's bark beneath my fingers. I scurried up the trunk, scrambled through the branches, and finally found an opening to another world. I didn't know which one it was until I tumbled out onto floor nineteen, right at Halfborn's feet.

"Mallory!" he yelled. "I've been looking all over for you, woman! You are the most reckless, foolhardy einherji—"

I got to my feet and glared at him. Then I hurled myself into his arms. "Oh yeah?" I murmured against his bare chest. "Well . . . takes one to know one."

VANAHEIM

Well, That Was a Surprise

BY HALFBORN GUNDERSON

SOMEONE STOOD in the hallway outside my door. I tensed. Waiting. Listening.

Knock-knock. Knock. Knock-knock-knock.

That was the sign. I opened the door. "Get in. Quickly."

Alex Fierro skirted past me with a bundled-up towel in his arms. I glanced up and down the hallway, then closed the door. I turned to find Alex rolling his eyes.

"I still can't believe you made me use a secret knock." He handed me the towel, then dusted off his pink cashmere sweater vest and lime-green pants.

I showed him a mangled slice of pizza. "Mallory tried to get in a few minutes ago. I had to be sure it was you and not her coming back to trash the place."

"Yeah, your peephole wouldn't work at all."

"Oh. I forgot about that. Anyway."

I led him into my arts-and-crafts room. That's right—arts and crafts. There's more to me than just fighting to the death. I'd started with the basics—finger paints and macaroni sculptures, glitter glue on paper hearts, string art and coat-hanger mobiles—and worked my way up to finer artistic endeavors.

Alex gaped when he saw my latest project. "Dude. It's *huge.*"

I shrugged. "Go big or go home, right?"

The project was a mosaic for Mallory made from an assortment of found and recycled objects: weapon fragments, pebbles from different worlds, shards of shattered glass. Alex, floor nineteen's resident potter, had brought me pieces of broken pottery, which he'd handcrafted by hurling unsatisfactory pots against a wall.

I unrolled the towel and inspected the shards. "These are perfect. Thanks. Now I just need Vanir dragon scales."

"Why Vanir dragons?" Alex wanted to know.

"They're red, yellow, and orange—perfect for battlefield flames, blood, and gore. See, I'm depicting Mallory's and my first battle together."

"Aw, Halfborn." Alex chucked me under the chin. "You're a romantic!"

"I'm also behind schedule. I want to give it to her on the battle's anniversary next week. I gotta get to Vanaheim and back before Mallory really *does* break down my door."

Alex uncoiled his garrote from his belt. "Want a wingman?"

"Nah. I got this." I opened a closet full of weapons and selected an ax and a shield from my collection. "Could you stay here, though, and make sure Mallory doesn't get in?"

Alex grimaced. "I'd rather fight a dragon than face your angry girlfriend, but sure, I'll hang out here until you get back."

"Thanks. I owe you one."

Alex smiled. "I'll take you up on that sometime."

Weapons securely in place over my TOUGH MUDDER T-shirt—I love those Midgard obstacle-course challenges—I made my way through the hotel hallways to the kitchen and the enormous walk-in refrigerator in the feast hall food-prep area. The quickest way to Vanaheim was via fresh produce. I went feetfirst into the potato bin and landed at the bottom of a gentle rolling hill in Folkvanger, the Vanir realm of the afterlife.

I surveyed my surroundings. The hill was covered with sweet-smelling wildflowers and dancing butterflies awash in warm, glowing light—the power of Freya, goddess and ruler of Vanaheim, washing over the realm. On the hilltop, Freya's handpicked warriors lounged on blankets, laughing and sipping chai.

I scowled. Peace, butterflies, chai: this world was awful.

Eeeeeeeeeee!

A high-pitched trumpet blast suddenly pierced the air. A cry to battle! My berserker instincts kicked in as if someone had flipped an ON switch. With a mighty roar, I tore off my TOUGH MUDDER tee and charged up the hill.

Nothing I'd ever encountered in Asgard prepared me for what came next.

The trumpet blast segued into a soft jazz tune. Brush drumsticks shushed out a whispered rhythm while other instruments—a piano, a clarinet, a bass guitar—wove a melody of notes through the air. The lilting music rolled over me like warm syrup on a stack of Sunday brunch pancakes.

It was horrible. I dropped my ax, fell to my knees, and clutched my ears.

"Whoa, buddy! You okay?" A dark-haired girl in a bikini top and sarong stared over at me with concern. She poked her blanket-mate with her elbow. "Hey. I think this dude needs some herbal supplements."

"No!" I stumbled to my feet. "I'm fine. Just point me toward Sessrumnir, and I'll be on my way."

"You'll miss the clarinet improv solo," she warned.

I shuddered. "No, I really won't."

The girl shrugged. "Your loss. Freya's palace is down the hill, past the volleyball court. Keep calm and bebop on!"

"Who was that?" I heard her friend ask as I hurried away.

"From the looks of him, I'd say someone who likes"—she lowered her voice to an embarrassed whisper—"polka music."

(She wasn't wrong. Give me a good oompah band over what they were listening to any day.)

I continued on to Sessrumnir, Freya's upside-down ship/palace of gold and silver, to seek the goddess's permission to hunt the dragons of her land. Inside, warriors lined the aisle to Freya's throne. Dozing warriors in hammocks, that is. Freya's throne was empty.

I shook a sleeping blond man in an unbuttoned Hawaiian shirt, tattered Bermuda shorts, and Birkenstock sandals. "Wake up. Where's Freya?"

The guy blinked sleepily. "Who are you?"

"Halfborn. Where's the goddess?"

"Halfborn." The guy said my name like he was testing it out. "What's that short for?"

"Nothing."

He chuckled in amazement. "Halfborn is short for Nothing? It's so *weird* how names work, isn't it?" He stuck out his hand. "I'm Miles. And sorry to be the bearer of bad news, but Freya's not here right now. I'd be super-pumped to help you out, though. Speaking of super-pumped"—he pointed to my bulging biceps and six-pack abs—"did you get ripped like that by going vegan?"

I ignored his question and got right to my own. "Whose permission do I need to hunt your dragons? I need some of their scales."

Miles scratched his head in confusion. "Hunt our dragons? Dude, they sleep harder than our warriors do. I mean, it'd take something pretty substantial to wake them up. You want scales, just walk up and take them."

Most people would have been relieved when a potentially deadly task turned out to be non-life-threatening. I am not most people. I prefer to earn things, not have them handed to me. Still, I'd come for dragon scales, so I set my disappointment aside.

"Where are the caves of these sleeping dragons, then?"

"Caves." Miles laughed. "You're really not from around here, are you?"

"No." *Thank the gods,* I added silently.

Miles spread his arms out wide and looked up. "Our dragons slumber under the open sky, basking in the light of Freya." He dropped his arms. "Come on, I'll take you there."

"No! I mean, you could just point the way."

"It's no trouble, man. Follow me."

I gritted my teeth. "Super."

Miles led me toward a distant canyon of soft red-gold sandstone. "I know! Let's take this opportunity to get to know one another better."

"Let's not and say we did."

"I'll go first," Miles continued. "My favorite flower is the daisy. It's just so darned cheerful! Do you have a favorite flower, Halfborn?"

"No."

"Oh, come on, now." He glanced at me sideways. "You must like tulips. Everyone likes tulips. Know why?"

"No."

"Because without tulips, you couldn't kiss!" He whooped and shoulder-bumped me. "Get it? Tulips? Like, *two lips*?" He made kissy sounds.

I nearly unleashed a heavy dose of berserk on him. Instead, I said, "There is one plant I admire. The Venus flytrap."

Miles nodded enthusiastically. "Interesting! Why that one, exactly?"

I turned on him. "Because it attacks its prey and then slowly and painfully consumes it."

That shut him up.

We reached the canyon. The wind had carved one side into wavy ledges that hung over the floor like shade canopies. Four dragons—one gold, one red, and two orange—snored in a hollow at the bottom, their scales glowing in the Freya light. Their wings were tucked in tight to their serpentine bodies. White smoke puffed from their nostrils like balls of cotton.

In other words, the dragons were non-life-threatening. Helping myself to their scales would be a piece of cake.

"I hate cake," I murmured as I started down the incline. Lucky me—Miles came along.

We were halfway down when a figure barreled over the canyon's edge on the far side.

Miles blinked. "Hey, that's Thor. And he's— Oh!"

Thor charged straight through the dragons.

Apparently, being kicked by a thunder god constitutes *something pretty substantial.* The dragons awoke with loud snorts. The clan erupted in chaos. Powerful wings flapping, the foursome took to the air, screeching in fury.

I darted beneath a sandstone overhang.

"Ooh, pretty!" Miles shaded his eyes and pointed at the dragons.

"Are you crazy?" I yelled. "Take cover!"

Miles waved his hand dismissively. "No need, my friend. The dragons would never attack the honored dead of Folkvanger. Doing so would disrupt the peace of the realm. They'll just fly around a bit and then go back to sleep." Then a look of mild concern crossed his face. "Of course, you're not one of Freya's chosen slain. If they're hungry and they smell you— Oh, look. There's something you don't see every day."

"What?"

"Fire breath."

I flung my shield up in front of me just as the orange dragons swooped past my overhang. Their flames superheated the metal but didn't touch me. They flew on and circled back for another pass.

This is more like it, I thought.

I leaped out and went to rip off my TOUGH MUDDER tee. Then I remembered that I'd ripped it off earlier, so I went straight to going berserk.

I raced down to the canyon floor. One orange dragon

NIDAVELLIR

ASGARD

landed next to me. A few well-placed swings of my ax took it out of commission permanently. I dodged a burst of fire from the second orange one, then darted in and whacked off its head.

"Doused that flame!" I cried.

"Dude!" Miles was scrambling out of the canyon. "You've got anger issues!"

"I know!"

The cranberry-red dragon gave a shriek of rage and dive-bombed me. It came a little too close for comfort. *Its* comfort, that is. I delivered a knockout blow to its nose with my shield, then cleaved its skull in two.

"Bring it on!" I bellowed.

The last dragon was by far the biggest. Its glinting gold scales nearly blinded me as it rushed in for the kill. I sidestepped, leaped onto its back, and rode it into the annoyingly beautiful Freya-light–drenched sky. The dragon bucked, writhed, and barrel-rolled, trying to unseat me. I put my ax handle across its throat and pulled back hard. It gasped and clawed at the handle, but I hung on tight. Then it stopped thrashing and spun in a slow death spiral to the canyon floor.

Boom! Its body kicked up a cloud of sand.

"Aaahhhrrrr!" Roaring in triumphant glory, I leaped off and pounded my shield with my ax.

"Dude. Whoa."

I looked up to find Miles staring at me openmouthed in

astonishment. Around him was a crowd of Vanaheim warriors. A few shifted and murmured uneasily.

The dark-haired girl in the bikini top moved forward. "They're . . . dead." A tear traced down her cheek.

It occurred to me then that while she, Miles, and the rest of Freya's chosen were technically warriors, they might never have seen an actual battle, let alone been in one.

"Well, yes, they're dead," I said carefully. "But if they'd succeeded in charbroiling and eating me, then *I'd* be dead. For good."

The girl looked at me blankly.

"Because I'm an einherji."

The girl still looked puzzled.

"If I die outside Valhalla, I stay dead. Unlike the dragons who, being mythical creatures, will vanish into Ginnungagap and eventually be reborn."

The girl's face cleared. "The dragons will be reborn?" She grabbed her friend's hands and started jumping up and down and squealing. "We'll have baby dragons here soon. *Soooo* cute!" She beamed at me. "Thank you so much for killing them!"

"Yeah. Don't mention it."

Miles came forward then. He looked from the dragons' hacked-up and pulverized bodies to my ax and sweaty, blood-streaked torso. Then he looked down at his own rangy frame and back to the bodies. He nodded with understanding.

ALFHEIM

JOTUNHEIM

HELHEIM

NIFLHEIM

VANAHEIM

MUSPELLHEIM

"So . . . your secret is the caveman paleo diet, not vegan-ism, huh?"

I thumped my chest. "Caveman paleo all the way, my man. Now if you'll excuse me." I hefted my ax and raked some scales from each dragon onto my shield. "I have a mosaic to finish."

MUSPELLHEIM

I Play with Fire

BY ALEX FIERRO

"AWWW, YOU two are so cute together it makes me sick. So I'm going back to my own room."

I'm not sure Mallory and Halfborn even heard me when I left, they were lip-locking so hard. Seeing them like that almost made me miss Magnus. Almost.

He was away visiting his cousin, Annabeth Chase. She'd advised him to leave his magic sword, Jack—aka Sumarbrander, the Sword of Summer—with me. So, while Mallory and Halfborn were smooching, I returned to my room to hang out with a talking blade.

Jack was slumbering on the decorative sword stand Blitzen had recently handcrafted for him. At least, I think he was slumbering. Hard to tell with a sword. No eyes.

I'd been working on a new pot when Halfborn had called looking for some shards. Now I returned to my wheel. As I worked the slick spinning clay under my fingers, I felt myself undergo a subtle shift.

I'd been identifying as male when I was with Mallory and Halfborn, and earlier, when I was with Samirah and her fiancé, Amir. Now I was female. And yes, the change really is that simple sometimes. Hence the term *gender fluid*.

I was deep into my new pot when Jack suddenly leaped up from his stand. The runes running down his blade pulsed an alarming red.

"*Señor! Señor!*" he cried. Then he paused as if looking at me. Again, hard to tell because of the whole no-eyes thing. Regardless, he picked up on my gender change. "Sorry. *Señorita! Señorita!*"

"Jack, chill. Take a breath. Wait. . . . Do you breathe?"

"No time for that now! I just heard a rumor via the underground weapon network that Surt, the fire lord of Muspellheim, is hatching a new nefarious plot!"

"Oh my gods!" I cried. "There's an underground weapon network?"

"Of course there is!" Jack retorted. "Think about it. What's the one thing all Nine Worlds have in common?"

"Thor's footprints and lingering fart stench?"

"Well . . . yes. But the answer I was looking for is *weap-ons*. And we talk. Gossip, really, if you want to know the truth. So, I heard the rumor about Surt from your garrote, who heard it from an arrow in Alfheim, who heard it from a mace in Jotunheim, who heard it from a vegetable peeler in Vanaheim, who—"

"A vegetable peeler?"

Jack shuddered. "Hope that you never hear a carrot screaming as it is being flayed by that dread instrument of torture, *chica*. Anyway, the communiqué traces all the way back to Muspellheim."

From the way he was slicing back and forth through the air, I could see that Jack was truly agitated. I was afraid he might pop a rune or something if I didn't start taking him seriously. Plus, Magnus trusted Jack with his life—literally—so that meant I trusted Jack, too.

I went to the bathroom sink to wash my hands. "Okay, what is Surt's plot?"

Jack sank his pommel down onto my couch and leaned his blade back against the cushions. "I don't have the details. But if it's Surt, it can't be good."

"So what are we waiting for?" I dried my hands on a towel embroidered with the hotel's initials, HV, then tossed it in the general direction of the hamper. "Sheath up and let's hit the tree."

"No! I can't go! I—I won't be able to resist the Black One."

Jack sounded miserable, and I remembered something Magnus had told me, about how, come Ragnarok, the Black One was destined to wield Jack and free Fenris Wolf. When they last encountered Surt, Jack had felt the pull of destiny and practically leaped out of Magnus's grasp to join the fire lord. If Jack came near Surt again without Magnus there to hold him back . . .

"Hey, no, of course you can't," I said hurriedly. "You stay here, safe and sound and Surt-free. Sam's back from her special assignment, so I'll grab her, and we'll get Hearth and Blitz and—"

Jack flew to a few inches in front of my face, his runes flashing in a jarring disco-light display. "No! Surt can detect einherjar and elves, dwarves and Valkyries. You must do this alone."

I waved my hands in the air. "Um, hello? Aren't you forgetting one little detail? *I'm* an einherji. What's to prevent Surt from sniffing me out?"

Jack went quiet again. "Use your shape-shifting powers. You'll be okay if you keep changing form," he finally said. "Plus, your gender fluidity will throw him off. He won't be able to get a lock on you."

I raised an eyebrow. "No offense, but you don't sound too sure about that."

"I am sure! Well, pretty sure, anyway. Sort of."

Not exactly confidence-inducing. But I couldn't just sit around while the Black One hatched a sinister plan of some sort. I'd had enough of that kind of thing in my afterlife already, thank you very much. If there was a chance I could stop him before he started, I had to take it.

So I looped my special golden garrote—the one the goddess Sif had given to me—around my waist. I moved to my atrium, intending to climb through the World Tree until I hit an entrance to Muspellheim, but Jack stopped me.

"Take the service elevator," he advised. "I hear the captain of the Valkyries once got blowtorched when the doors opened, so it must lead right to Muspellheim."

That tidbit of info gave me pause. "Quick question, disco sword: What's to keep me from being turned into einherji flambé when I use that elevator? Or while I'm roaming through Muspellheim, for that matter?"

"Um . . . any chance your sweater vest is fire-resistant?"

"No. It's cashmere."

"Oh. Well, I'm out of ideas."

I was too, until my gaze landed on my kiln. Gas fueled, it looked like a steel trash can with squat legs and a pop-up lid. The interior could reach temperatures northward of two thousand degrees—perfect for turning squishy clay pots into hard-baked earthenware. A thick layer of ceramic insulation protected me and my room from the extreme heat.

With a bit of magic, I thought, *I bet I could transform some of those fibers into something that will shield me from Muspellheim's fire.*

I was no rune master like Hearthstone, but I was no stranger to magic, either. When I was alive, my mom, Loki (don't ask), had taught me an enchantment that turned my clay-cutter into a deadly garrote. More recently, I'd brought a ceramic warrior named Pottery Barn to life with just a touch of my fingers.

To create my shape-shifting fire shield, I combined a handful of fibers with my signature Urnes symbol—intertwined snakes that represented flexibility—and an *algiz* stone I hastily borrowed without asking from Hearthstone's rune bag. (If he didn't want me to take it, then why did he leave his room unlocked?) I focused on turning the three things into an invisible membrane that surrounded me like a second skin.

To my delight—okay, amazement—it worked. Even better, the membrane changed shape when I did. In the ultimate test, I fired up the kiln, turned into a housefly, and, with Jack hovering anxiously nearby, plunged inside. I emerged completely unsinged.

It was time to get going. "Stay safe, disco sword."

Jack bobbed over to my potted snake plant and hid in the broad, sword-shaped leaves. "You too."

I turned into an ant on the short elevator ride down to Muspellheim. A blast of fire engulfed me when the doors opened. If not for my membrane, I would have exploded like a kernel of unpopped corn.

"Nice welcome," I muttered.

Judging by the opulent surroundings—gold- and ebony-paneled walls, vaulted ceilings that glowed like embers, and several red, orange, and black silk tapestries depicting the same handsome but cruel man lording over dancing fire demons—I hadn't landed in some obscure Nowheresville but right in the heart of Surt's palace itself.

I squared my thorax with determination. *Okay. Time to get crawling!*

After going about five feet in ten minutes, I came to my senses and changed into a housefly. I made much better time after that.

I found the Black One in a large meeting room. Elegant, long-fingered hands clasped behind his back, not a single black hair out of place, he stood staring out a huge picture window at the fiery landscape below. Seated at the table were several gods and goddesses I didn't recognize. So how did I know they were deities? They weren't covered in flames, so they weren't fire giants or demons. They weren't bothered by the heat, either—no screaming or sizzling or burning to a crispy crunch. Logical conclusion? They were immortals.

Surt turned, and I had to choke back a laugh. With his black-on-black-on-black attire, equally black features, and fierce black expression, he should have been intimidating. But his nose was so tiny—he was growing a new one, Magnus having sliced off his old snout in an earlier encounter—that he came off as more ridiculous than fearsome.

The lord of fire moved with the grace of a ballroom dancer to stand at the head of the table. He pressed his fingertips to the surface. The room quieted. Then Surt spoke—and suddenly, he didn't seem so ridiculous any-more. His deep voice thrummed in my mind, pushing at my thoughts as if trying to replace them with his own. Swaying me to his way of thinking.

No wonder Jack was so desperate to go to him, I thought. *If the deities fall under his spell . . .*

Luckily, my willpower has withstood an even greater manipulator: my mother, Loki. (Again, don't ask.) Carefully, so as not to draw attention to myself, I pushed back against Surt's voice. Its power slowly ebbed away until my mind was once again my own, and I could listen to his words.

"Odin, Thor, Frey, Loki," Surt said. "They're all so focused on the coming of Ragnarok that they've forgotten what comes afterward. A new world!" He raised his arms and stood silhouetted against the picture window. "A new world will emerge when the floodwaters recede, the fires die, the ice storms melt, and the earthquakes cease!"

He dropped his arms and his voice, and leaned forward on the table again. "That world will need gods, my friends. You could be those gods. You, who Odin and his lot have forgotten, could take their places . . . *if* I deem you worthy of fighting on the right side of the war come Ragnarok. *My side.*"

While Surt was orating, I studied the deities. They were a mixed bag, some ancient-looking and in traditional Viking garb, others more youthful and wearing clothes from more recent centuries. Their appearances gave no indication of their identity, making me long for the name tags worn by the Hotel Valhalla staff. Whoever they were, they were hanging on Surt's every word.

Then Surt abruptly stopped talking. Frowning, he lifted his chin. His nostrils flared. Then he swung his head around and zeroed in on my hiding spot.

I swore silently. I'd forgotten to keep changing shape, and the fire lord had sniffed me out. I couldn't shape-shift now, not with Surt staring directly at me.

A chair scraped the floor. "What the blue blazes is that?" a goddess cried in astonishment. I assumed she had spotted me, but then she and the others rushed to the window. One jostled Surt. When he turned to glare at the offender, I shape-shifted into a flea and leaped to another location.

From my new vantage point, I had a perfect view of the disturbance outside. Thor was running past, sweating bullets and yelling "Ow-ow-ow-ow-ow" with every footfall. And no wonder—the ground in Muspellheim was covered in lava (and not the pretend kind like in the leap-on-the-furniture-don't-touch-the-lava game).

Surt stalked to the window. I expected him to open it and blast Thor with a fireball, but he just yanked the black silk drapes shut. "Show's over," he barked. "*If* you would all resume your seats, you may now state your worthiness to join me at Ragnarok."

The first god stood up. Balding, sweaty, with a stomach that protruded over his belt, he reminded me of a foreman on a low-budget infrastructure project.

"THE NAME'S HOLLER!" he bellowed. "GOD OF DISEASE, DESTRUCTION, AND DISASTER! LET ME PLAY FOR YOUR TEAM, AND I WILL STRIKE DOWN THE MASSES WITH DEVASTATING HEAD COLDS! THEN I'LL FOLLOW UP WITH A LEAKY-FAUCET EPIDEMIC AND A RASH OF TEETH-RATTLING POTHOLES!"

"Interesting." Surt scratched a few notes on a yellow legal pad. "Next?"

A pinched-faced spinster type with ramrod-straight posture rose from her chair and smoothed out her pinafore. "I am Snotra."

Once again, I almost gave myself away by laughing. I changed into a cockroach—for some reason, I was defaulting to bugs—and skittered beneath a sideboard.

Snotra reminded the others that she was the goddess of prudence and self-discipline. "I will make sure the giants attack in an orderly fashion. No cutting the line. No horsing around. No"—she drew herself up and tightened her thin lips disapprovingly—"gum-chewing. And I will organize a chore chart of post-Ragnarok duties."

"Mmm," Surt murmured. "Quite . . . fastidious of you."

The other deities stood up in turn. Some, like Snotra and Holler, had actual plans to propose. The rest were prepared to throw in with Surt because they had grievances with the current gods in power.

Forseti, the cigar-smoking god of justice, complained about not being part of Odin's inner circle. "The All-Fadda kept me outta the big decisions, like where and how to tie up Loki, you know? I'm with you, though, new world comes, and then *boom!* I'll be the big cheese in charge—present company excluded, of course, my lord," he added hurriedly when Surt frowned.

The goddess Glum, who looked and sounded exactly like her name, was one of Frigg's handmaidens. "I'm just so *tired* of being in her shadow all the time," she said. "I want to have a chance to shine."

"And what would you do if given that chance?" Surt prodded.

Glum stared at him. "Do?"

A goddess in a dowdy shirt and shapeless skirt cupped Glum's face in her hand and gave it an affectionate shake. "Pretty young thing like you, you don't need to *do*. You need someone to do *for* you. A husband!" She glanced over at Forseti, then leaned close to Glum. "I'm Lofn," she whispered, "goddess of arranged marriages." She handed her a business card. "Call me. We'll talk."

More gods and goddesses introduced themselves. I hadn't heard of any of them, which made me a little sad. I know what it's like to be pushed aside. It stinks.

And yet, with each new deity that spoke, my tension grew.

They might be a motley crew, I reminded myself, *but they still add to Surt's power.*

I had to get them to come back to our side. Or at least not join his. But how?

Surt began detailing his plans for his new world order. Once again, the deities fell under the spell of his hypnotic voice. I had to find a way to break that spell.

Then it hit me: I'd put a bug in their ears. Literally.

I changed into a gnat and flew near Snotra. "Surt thrives in chaos," I whispered in her ear. "Do you really think he'll let you create order?"

To Holler, I murmured, "What place will a god of destruction have in a new world, where the goal is to build?"

"Surt will expect something from you," I breathed in Glum's ear. "Do you really want that kind of pressure?"

Around the table I went, sowing whispered seeds of dissent. When I'd finished, the deities were looking at Surt with suspicion.

The Black One sensed the change in attitude. He slowly rose from his seat. "My friends, you have outlined what you have to offer. Now perhaps you need a reminder of what *I* bring to the table."

He thrust his hand in the air and summoned his sword of pure white flame. The gods and goddesses cowered. Throwing his head back and laughing, Surt grew to his full

giant size. "You minor, forgotten, *pathetic* deities! So easy
to bend to my will. Not one of you would dare to defy me!"

I chose that moment to shape-shift into a bee, buzz up
Surt's teeny-tiny nose, and jab him with my stinger.

With a howl of pain, Surt dropped his sword and shrank
to his previous size. I changed into my true form.

"*I* dare."

I whipped one end of my golden garrote around his
neck and yanked it tight. Then I snatched up his flame
sword and with one upward flick, sliced off his pubescent
nose. "Jack and Magnus send their regards."

Surt lunged for me. I transformed into a bighorn sheep
and head-butted him right where his nose used to be. Then
I changed back to human, tightened the garrote until
his eyes bulged, and threatened him with his own sword.
"Come at me again," I warned, "and you'll regret it."

I surveyed the stunned deities. "If one einherji can
do this, imagine what all of us can do. And *will* do, come
Ragnarok. We are not destined to win, but we will fight with
honor. We would welcome you on our side of the fight. But,
if you must side with him"—I gave the garrote a vicious tug
and was rewarded with a gurgle from Surt—"know this: I
will personally hunt you down on the Last Battlefield of
Vigridr and see that you are sent straight to Ginnungagap.
The choice is yours."

The deities vanished.

I nodded. "Yeah, that's what I thought."

I admit it: I was feeling a bit full of myself. Then I realized my predicament. I couldn't return to Valhalla, not with Surt wrapped in my garrote. Odin frowns on bringing nasties like him into his realm. And if I let Surt go, he'd attack me—the flaming rage in his eyes made that pretty clear.

I was starting to panic—just a little—when I heard a distant *ding*. Sam, Hearth, Blitz, Halfborn, T.J., and Mallory charged in, weapons drawn and ready, only to skid to a halt when they saw me with Surt on a leash and his sword in my hand.

"Hey, guys," I said. "How is it you're not burned to a crisp?"

"A little elfish shielding magic." Sam nodded at Hearth. Arms raised wide overhead, the elf's face was contorted with effort. "Good thing he had a spare algiz rune, or we'd all be toast."

"Why'd you come here, though?" I asked. "Not that I'm not glad to see you. Just confused."

"Jack told us you were in trouble," T.J. said. "He heard it from a billy club, who heard it from a slingshot, who heard it from your garrote."

"And speaking of garrotes," Mallory added, eyeing the wire digging into Surt's throat, "it seems you don't need our help after all."

"Actually, I could use some assistance," I admitted.

"Got just what you need, right here." Blitzen stepped forward holding a thin silvery rope. "Nowhere near the same quality as Gleipnir or the new rope holding Fenris Wolf, but it'll do in a pinch."

While he hog-tied Surt with some sweet cowboy roping moves, Sam turned to me. "What the Helheim happened here, anyway?"

"Long story. I'll tell you in the elevator."

"Then if we're all ready, after you, little . . . erm . . ." Halfborn looked me over. "Lady?"

I grinned. "Got it in one."

We headed to the doorway. At the last moment, I flicked my garrote free from Surt's neck. Then I held up his sword. "I'm keeping this. Souvenir of our special time together. And one more thing. The next time you try plotting against us, remember this."

I gestured to my friends.

"We'll be ready."

Goal Achieved!
Sort of . . .

BY THOR

ASGARD. MIDGARD. Nidavellir. Alfheim. Jotunheim. Helheim. Niflheim. Vanaheim. Muspellheim. Trekking through the Nine Worlds to rack up ten million steps wasn't easy. The chafing and blisters alone nearly ended my quest to earn a cameo on my favorite Midgard television show. But I'd do it all over again if I had to.

Which, apparently, I will have to, because I forgot to turn on my FitnessKnut.

GLOSSARY

AESIR—gods of war, close to humans

ALFHEIM—the home of the light elves, ruled by the god Frey

ASGARD—the home of the Aesir

BALDER—god of light, the second son of Odin and Frigg, and twin brother of Hod. Frigg made all earthly things swear to never harm her son, but she forgot about mistletoe. Loki tricked Hod into killing Balder with a dart made of mistletoe.

BEAR GRYLLS—a British adventurer best known for his television series *Man vs. Wild*

BIFROST—the rainbow bridge leading from Asgard to Midgard

BOUDICA—a queen of the British Celtic Iceni tribe who led a revolt against occupying Romans in 61 CE

EINHERJAR (EINHERJI, sing.)—great heroes who have died with bravery on Earth; soldiers in Odin's eternal army; they train in Valhalla for Ragnarok, when the bravest of them will join Odin against Loki and the giants in the battle at the end of the world

FENRIS WOLF—an invulnerable wolf born of Loki's affair with a giantess; his mighty strength strikes fear even in the gods, who keep him tied to a rock on an island. He is destined to break free on the day of Ragnarok.

FIMBULWINTER—three years of unending winter immediately preceding Ragnarok

FOLKVANGER—the Vanir afterlife for slain heroes, ruled by the goddess Freya

FORSETI—god of justice

FREY—the god of spring and summer; the sun, the rain, and the harvest; abundance and fertility, growth and vitality. Frey is the twin brother of Freya and, like his sister, is associated with great beauty. He is the lord of Alfheim.

FREYA—the goddess of love; twin sister of Frey; ruler of Folkvanger

FRIGG—goddess of marriage and motherhood; Odin's wife and the queen of Asgard; mother of Balder and Hod

GARM—the guard dog of Hel

GINNUNGAGAP—the primordial void; a mist that obscures appearances

GJALLAR—Heimdall's horn

GLAMOUR—illusion magic

GLEIPNIR—a rope made by dwarves to keep Fenris Wolf in bondage

GLUM—a minor goddess, a handmaiden of Frigg

GUNGNIR—Odin's staff

HEIDRUN—the goat in the Tree of Laeradr whose milk is brewed for the magical mead of Valhalla

HEIMDALL—god of vigilance and the guardian of Bifrost, the gateway to Asgard

HEL—goddess of the dishonorable dead; born of Loki's affair with a giantess

HELHEIM—the underworld, ruled by Hel and inhabited by those who died in wickedness, old age, or illness

HLADGUNNR—daughter of Hel; granddaughter of Loki; a Valkyrie that played tricks on her victims

HLIDSKJALF—the High Seat of Odin

HOD—Balder's blind brother

HOLLER—Norse god of disease, destruction, and disaster

HONIR—the Aesir god of indecision, avoidance, and mystery

HULDER—a domesticated forest sprite

HVERGELMIR—the hot springs surrounding Yggdrasil

JOTUN—giant

JOTUNHEIM—realm of the earth giants

LOFN—goddess of arranged marriages

LOKI—god of mischief, magic, and artifice; the son of two giants, Farbauti and Laufey; adept with magic and shape-shifting. He is alternately malicious and heroic to the Asgardian gods and to humankind. Because of his role in the death of Balder, Loki was chained by Odin to three giant boulders with a poisonous serpent coiled over his head. The venom of the snake occasionally irritates Loki's face, and his writhing can cause earthquakes.

LYNGVI—the Isle of Heather, where Fenris Wolf is bound

MIDGARD—realm of the humans

MIMIR—an Aesir god who, along with Honir, traded places with Vanir gods Frey and Njord at the end of the war between the Aesir and the Vanir. When the Vanir didn't like his counsel, they cut off his head and sent it to Odin. Odin placed the head in a magical well, where the water brought it back to life, and Mimir soaked up all the knowledge of the World Tree.

MJOLNIR—Thor's hammer

MUSPELLHEIM—the home of the fire giants and demons

NÁBRÓK—pants made out of a corpse's skin

NIDAVELLIR—the home of the dwarves

NIDHOGG—the dragon that lives at the bottom of the World Tree and chews on its roots

NIFLHEIM—the world of ice, fog, and mist

ODIN—the "All-Father" and king of the gods; the god of war and death, but also poetry and wisdom. By trading one eye for a drink from the Well of Wisdom, Odin gained unparalleled knowledge. He has the ability to observe all the Nine Worlds from his throne in Asgard; in addition to his great hall, he also resides in Valhalla with the bravest of those slain in battle.

RAGNAROK—the Day of Doom or Judgment, when the bravest of the einherjar will join Odin against Loki and the giants in the battle at the end of the world

RATATOSK—an invulnerable squirrel that constantly runs up and down the World Tree carrying insults between the eagle that lives at the top and Nidhogg, the dragon that lives at the roots

SAEHRIMNIR—the magical beast of Valhalla; every day it is

killed and cooked for dinner and every morning it is resur-
rected; it tastes like whatever the diner wants

SESSRUMNIR—the Hall of Many Seats, Freya's mansion in
Folkvanger

SIERSGRUNNR—Norse for *cheesebutt*

SIF—goddess of the earth; mother of Uller by her first husband; Thor is her second husband; the rowan is her sacred
tree

SNOTRA—goddess of prudence and self-discipline

SUMARBRANDER—the Sword of Summer

SURT—lord of Muspellheim

THANE—a lord of Valhalla

THOR—god of thunder; son of Odin. Thunderstorms are
the earthly effects of Thor's mighty chariot rides across the
sky, and lightning is caused by hurling his great hammer,
Mjolnir.

TREE OF LAERADR—a tree in the center of the Feast Hall of
the Slain in Valhalla containing immortal animals that have
particular jobs

TYR—god of courage, law, and trial by combat; he lost a hand
to Fenris's bite when the Wolf was restrained by the gods

UTGARD-LOKI—the most powerful sorcerer of Jotunheim;
king of the mountain giants

VALHALLA—paradise for warriors in the service of Odin

VALKNUT—a Norse design of three interlocked triangles;
the word comes from *vair*, meaning *slain warriors*, and *knut*,
meaning *knot*

VALKYRIE—Odin's handmaidens, who choose slain heroes
to bring to Valhalla

VANAHEIM—the home of the Vanir

VANIR—gods of nature; close to elves

VIGRIDR—a plain that will be the site of the battle between
the gods and Surt's forces during Ragnarok

YGGDRASIL—the World Tree

PRONUNCIATION GUIDE

AESIR	*AY-ser*
ALFHEIM	*ALF-haym*
ALGIZ	*AL-gheets*
ASGARD	*AZ-gahrrd*
BALDER	*BALL-der*
BIFROST	*BEE-frrohst*
DAGAZ	*DAH-gahz*
EINHERJAR/EINHERJI	*in-HAIRR-yar/in-HAIRR-yee*
EITRI	*EE-tree*
FENRIS	*FEHN-rrihss*
FIMBULWINTER	*FEEM-bool-ween-ter*
FOLKVANGER	*FOHK-vahn-ger*
FORSETI	*FORR-seh-tee*
FREY	*FRRAY*
FREYA	*FRRAY-uh*
FRIGG	*FRRIHG*
GARM	*GAHRRM*
GEBO	*GIH-bo*
GINNUNGAGAP	*GEEN-un-guh-gahp*
GLEIPNIR	*GLYP-neer*
GLUM	*GLOOM*
HAGALAZ	*HA-ga-lahts*
HEIDRUN	*HY-druhn*
HEIMDALL	*HAME-doll*
HEL	*HEHL*
HELGI	*HEL-ghee*

HELHEIM	*HEHL-haym*
HLADGUNNR	*H'LAHD-goo-ner*
HLIDSKJALF	*H'LIHD-skelf*
HOD	*rhymes with odd*
HOLLER	*HO-lair*
HUNDING	*HOON-deeng*
HVERGELMIR	*H'VERR-gehl-meer*
ISA	*EES-ah*
JOTUN	*YOH-toon*
JOTUNHEIM	*YOH-toon-haym*
KENAZ	*KEH-nahtz*
LAERADR	*LAY-rrah-dur*
LAGAZ	*lah-GAHTS*
LOFN	*LOH-fin*
LOKI	*LOH-kee*
LYNGVI	*LEENG-vee*
MIDGARD	*MIHD-gahrrd*
MIMIR	*MEE-meer*
MJOLNIR	*MEE'OHL-neer*
MUSPELLHEIM	*MOOS-pehl-haym*
NÁBRÓK	*NO-broke*
NIDAVELLIR	*Nee-duh-vehl-EER*
NIDHOGG	*NEED-hawg*
NIFLHEIM	*NIHF-uh-haym*
ODIN	*OH-dihn*
RAGNAROK	*RAG-nuh-rrawk*
RATATOSK	*RAT-uh-tawsk*
SAEHRIMNIR	*SAY-h'rrihm-neer*
SAMIRAH AL-ABBAS	*Sah-MEER-ah ahl-AH-bahss*
SESSRUMNIR	*SEHSS-rroom-neer*
SIERSGRUNNR	*Sears-grroon-ner*

SIF	*SEEV*
SNORRI	*SNOH-rree*
SNOTRA	*SNOH-trah*
SUMARBRANDER	*SOO-marr-brrand-der*
SURT	*SERT*
THOR	*THORE*
TIWAZ	*TEE-vahz*
TYR	*TEER*
URUZ	*OOR-oots*
UTGARD-LOKI	*OOT-gahrrd-LOH-kee*
VALHALLA	*Val-HAHL-uh*
VALKNUT	*valk-NOOT*
VALKYRIE	*VAL-kerr-ee*
VANAHEIM	*VAN-uh-haym*
VANIR	*Vah-NEER*
VIGRIDR	*VEE-grree-der*
YGGDRASIL	*IHG-drruh-sihl*

RUNES (IN ORDER OF MENTION)

DAGAZ—new beginnings, transformations

GEBO—gift

LAGAZ—water, liquefaction

ALGIZ—shielding

ISA—ice

URUZ—ox

HAGALAZ—hail

KENAZ—the torch

TIWAZ—the rune of Tyr

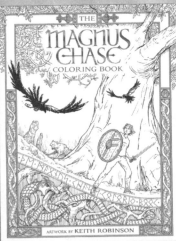
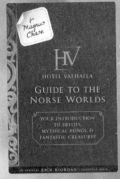

FROM *NEW YORK TIMES* BEST-SELLING AUTHOR
RICK RIORDAN

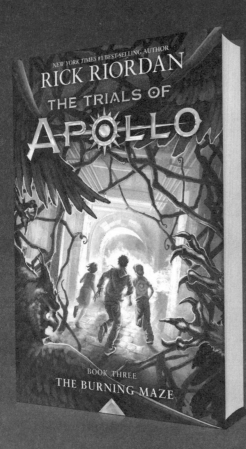

DON'T MISS THE TRIALS OF APOLLO
SERIES, FEATURING ALL YOUR
FAVORITE CHARACTERS FROM
THE HEROES OF OLYMPUS!

HERE'S A SNEAK PEEK AT BOOK ONE. . . .

1

Hoodlums punch my face
I would smite them if I could
Mortality blows

MY NAME IS APOLLO. I used to be a god.

In my four thousand six hundred and twelve years, I have done many things. I inflicted a plague on the Greeks who besieged Troy. I blessed Babe Ruth with three home runs in game four of the 1926 World Series. I visited my wrath upon Britney Spears at the 2007 MTV Video Music Awards.

But in all my immortal life, I never before crash-landed in a Dumpster.

I'm not even sure how it happened.

I simply woke up falling. Skyscrapers spiraled in and out of view. Flames streamed off my body. I tried to fly. I tried to change into a cloud or teleport across the world or do a hundred other things that should have been easy for me, but I just kept falling. I plunged into a narrow canyon between two buildings and BAM!

Is anything sadder than the sound of a god hitting a pile of garbage bags?

I lay groaning and aching in the open Dumpster. My nostrils burned with the stench of rancid bologna and used diapers. My ribs felt broken, though that shouldn't have been possible.

My mind stewed in confusion, but one memory floated to the surface—the voice of my father, Zeus: *YOUR FAULT. YOUR PUNISHMENT.*

I realized what had happened to me. And I sobbed in despair.

Even for a god of poetry such as myself, it is difficult to describe how I felt. How could you—a mere mortal—possibly understand? Imagine being stripped of your clothes, then blasted with a fire hose in front of a laughing crowd. Imagine the ice-cold water filling your mouth and lungs, the pressure bruising your skin, turning your joints to putty. Imagine feeling helpless, ashamed, completely vulnerable—publicly and brutally stripped of everything that makes you *you.* My humiliation was worse than that.

YOUR FAULT, Zeus's voice rang in my head.

"No!" I cried miserably. "No, it wasn't! Please!"

Nobody answered. On either side of me, rusty fire escapes zigzagged up brick walls. Above, the winter sky was gray and unforgiving.

I tried to remember the details of my sentencing. Had my father told me how long this punishment would last? What was I supposed to do to regain his favor?

My memory was too fuzzy. I could barely recall what Zeus looked like, much less why he'd decided to toss me to earth. There'd been a war with the giants, I thought. The gods had been caught off guard, embarrassed, almost defeated.

The only thing I knew for certain: my punishment was

unfair. Zeus needed someone to blame, so of course he'd picked the handsomest, most talented, most popular god in the pantheon: me.

I lay in the garbage, staring at the label inside the Dumpster lid: FOR PICK-UP, CALL 1-555-STENCHY.

Zeus will reconsider, I told myself. *He's just trying to scare me. Any moment, he will yank me back to Olympus and let me off with a warning.*

"Yes . . ." My voice sounded hollow and desperate. "Yes, that's it."

I tried to move. I wanted to be on my feet when Zeus came to apologize. My ribs throbbed. My stomach clenched. I clawed the rim of the Dumpster and managed to drag myself over the side. I toppled out and landed on my shoulder, which made a cracking sound against the asphalt.

"*Araggeeddeee,*" I whimpered through the pain. "Stand up. Stand up."

Getting to my feet was not easy. My head spun. I almost passed out from the effort. I stood in a dead-end alley. About fifty feet away, the only exit opened onto a street with grimy storefronts for a bail bondsman's office and a pawnshop. I was somewhere on the west side of Manhattan, I guessed, or perhaps Crown Heights, in Brooklyn. Zeus must have been really angry with me.

I inspected my new body. I appeared to be a teenaged Caucasian male, clad in sneakers, blue jeans, and a green polo shirt. How utterly *drab*. I felt sick, weak, and so, so human.

I will never understand how you mortals tolerate it. You live your entire life trapped in a sack of meat, unable to enjoy simple pleasures like changing into a hummingbird or dissolving into pure light.

And now, heavens help me, I was one of you—just another meat sack.

I fumbled through my pants pockets, hoping I still had the keys to my sun chariot. No such luck. I found a cheap nylon wallet containing a hundred dollars in American currency— lunch money for my first day as a mortal, perhaps—along with a New York State junior driver's license featuring a photo of a dorky, curly-haired teen who could not possibly be me, with the name *Lester Papadopoulos*. The cruelty of Zeus knew no bounds!

I peered into the Dumpster, hoping my bow, quiver, and lyre might have fallen to earth with me. I would have set-tled for my harmonica. There was nothing.

I took a deep breath. *Cheer up*, I told myself. *I must have retained some of my godly abilities. Matters could be worse.*

A raspy voice called, "Hey, Cade, take a look at this loser."

Blocking the alley's exit were two young men: one squat and platinum blond, the other tall and redheaded. Both wore oversize hoodies and baggy pants. Serpentine tattoo designs covered their necks. All they were missing were the words I'M A THUG printed in large letters across their foreheads.

The redhead zeroed in on the wallet in my hand. "Now, be nice, Mikey. This guy looks friendly enough." He grinned and pulled a hunting knife from his belt. "In fact, I bet he wants to give us all his money."

———

I blame my disorientation for what happened next.

I knew my immortality had been stripped away, but I still considered myself the mighty Apollo! One cannot change one's way of thinking as easily as one might, say, turn into a snow leopard.

Also, on previous occasions when Zeus had punished me by making me mortal (yes, it had happened twice before), I had retained massive strength and at least some of my godly powers. I assumed the same would be true now.

I was *not* going to allow two young mortal ruffians to take Lester Papadopoulos's wallet.

I stood up straight, hoping Cade and Mikey would be intimidated by my regal bearing and divine beauty. (Surely those qualities could not be taken from me, no matter what my driver's license photo looked like.) I ignored the warm Dumpster juice trickling down my neck.

"I am Apollo," I announced. "You mortals have three choices: offer me tribute, flee, or be destroyed."

I wanted my words to echo through the alley, shake the towers of New York, and cause the skies to rain smoking ruin. None of that happened. On the word *destroyed*, my voice squeaked.

The redhead Cade grinned even wider. I thought how amusing it would be if I could make the snake tattoos around his neck come alive and strangle him to death.

"What do you think, Mikey?" he asked his friend. "Should we give this guy tribute?"

Mikey scowled. With his bristly blond hair, his cruel small eyes, and his thick frame, he reminded me of the monstrous sow that terrorized the village of Crommyon back in the good old days.

"Not feeling the tribute, Cade." His voice sounded like he'd been eating lit cigarettes. "What were the other options?"

"Fleeing?" said Cade.

"Nah," said Mikey.

"Being destroyed?"

Mikey snorted. "How about we destroy *him* instead?"

Cade flipped his knife and caught it by the handle. "I can live with that. After you."

I slipped the wallet into my back pocket. I raised my fists. I did not like the idea of flattening mortals into flesh waffles, but I was sure I could do it. Even in my weakened state, I would be far stronger than any human.

"I warned you," I said. "My powers are far beyond your comprehension."

Mikey cracked his knuckles. "Uh-huh."

He lumbered forward.

As soon as he was in range, I struck. I put all my wrath into that punch. It should have been enough to vaporize Mikey and leave a thug-shaped impression on the asphalt.

Instead he ducked, which I found quite annoying.

I stumbled forward. I have to say that when Prometheus fashioned you humans out of clay he did a shoddy job. Mortal legs are clumsy. I tried to compensate, drawing upon my boundless reserves of agility, but Mikey kicked me in the back. I fell on my divine face.

My nostrils inflated like air bags. My ears popped. The

taste of copper filled my mouth. I rolled over, groaning, and found the two blurry thugs staring down at me.

"Mikey," said Cade, "are you comprehending this guy's power?"

"Nah," said Mikey. "I'm not comprehending it."

"Fools!" I croaked. "I will destroy you!"

"Yeah, sure." Cade tossed away his knife. "But first I think we'll stomp you."

Cade raised his boot over my face, and the world went black.

Also by Rick Riordan

PERCY JACKSON AND THE OLYMPIANS
Book One: *The Lightning Thief*
Book Two: *The Sea of Monsters*
Book Three: *The Titan's Curse*
Book Four: *The Battle of the Labyrinth*
Book Five: *The Last Olympian*

The Demigod Files

The Lightning Thief: The Graphic Novel
The Sea of Monsters: The Graphic Novel
The Titan's Curse: The Graphic Novel

Percy Jackson's Greek Gods
Percy Jackson's Greek Heroes
From Percy Jackson: Camp Half-Blood Confidential
The Percy Jackson Coloring Book
The Lightning Thief Illustrated Edition

THE KANE CHRONICLES
Book One: *The Red Pyramid*
Book Two: *The Throne of Fire*
Book Three: *The Serpent's Shadow*

The Red Pyramid: The Graphic Novel
The Throne of Fire: The Graphic Novel
The Serpent's Shadow: The Graphic Novel
From the Kane Chronicles: Brooklyn House Magicians' Manual

THE HEROES OF OLYMPUS
Book One: *The Lost Hero*
Book Two: *The Son of Neptune*
Book Three: *The Mark of Athena*
Book Four: *The House of Hades*
Book Five: *The Blood of Olympus*

ABOUT THE AUTHOR

RICK RIORDAN, dubbed "storyteller of the gods" by *Publishers Weekly*, is the author of five *New York Times* #1 best-selling series, including Magnus Chase and the Gods of Asgard, based on Norse myths. He is best known for his Percy Jackson and the Olympians books, which bring Greek mythology to life for contemporary readers. He expanded on that series with two more: the Heroes of Olympus and the Trials of Apollo, which cleverly combine Greek and Roman gods and heroes with his beloved modern characters. Rick tackled the ancient Egyptian gods in the magic-filled Kane Chronicles trilogy. Millions of fans across the globe have enjoyed his fast-paced and funny quest adventures as well as his two #1 best-selling myth collections, *Percy Jackson's Greek Gods* and *Percy Jackson's Greek Heroes*. Rick is also the publisher of an imprint at Disney Hyperion, Rick Riordan Presents, dedicated to finding other authors of highly entertaining fiction based on world cultures and mythologies. He lives in Boston, Massachusetts, with his wife and two sons. For more information, follow him on Twitter @camphalfblood.

Follow @ReadRiordan